LOST IN CYDONIA

TIMEBENDERS

#1. *Battle Before Time*

#2. *Doorway to Doom*

#3. *Invasion of the Time Troopers*

#4. *Lost in Cydonia*

Visit the author, Jim Denney, at
www.denneybooks.com/timebenders.html.

TIMEBENDERS

LOST IN CYDONIA

JIM DENNEY

Tommy
NELSON®

www.tommynelson.com

A Division of Thomas Nelson, Inc.
www.ThomasNelson.com

LOST IN CYDONIA

Published in Nashville, Tennessee, by Tommy Nelson®, a Division of Thomas Nelson, Inc.

Library of Congress Cataloging-in-Publication Data

Denney, James D.
    Lost in Cydonia / by Jim Denney.
        p. cm.— (Timebenders; #4)
    Summary: Max, Grady, Toby, and Allie and her father unexpectedly head for Mars in an antigravity orange Volkswagen named Timebender, where the Timelings help them learn more about God's will for their lives.
    ISBN 1-40030-042-8
    [1. Christian life—Fiction. 2. Space and time—Fiction. 3. Choice—Fiction. 4. Mars (Planet)—Fiction.] I. Title.
PZ7.D4272 Lo 2002
[Fic]—dc21   2002029545

Printed in the United States of America

03 04 05 06 PHX 5 4 3 2

To Bethany—
You make me laugh, you make me think,
you make me proud.

CONTENTS

1

THE SECRET

The planet Mars sparkled like a blood-red ruby against the blue star-frost of space.

The planet looks angry, thought Commander Thomas Wrye. *Angry and dangerous. When we get to Mars, we'll unlock one of the great secrets of the universe—an ancient riddle that has been waiting to be answered for thousands of years. And if the theories of some top scientists prove correct, what we find there just might destroy everything the human race has achieved.*

Clad in a pale blue jumpsuit, Commander Wrye floated weightlessly in a section of the International Space Station (ISS) called the Cupola. The Cupola was part of the Unity Node in the American section of the ISS. Large viewpanes surrounded the Cupola. From one viewpane, Commander Wrye could see Mars; from another, he had a spectacular view of planet Earth from two hundred fifty miles up; from another, he could see the nose section of Spaceship *Thuvia*, which was docked to Node Three, directly below the Cupola. Commander Wrye often came to the Cupola to gaze out into the universe, to think, to brood—and to worry about the mysterious secret that lurked on planet Mars. . . .

The commander's thoughts were interrupted by a clanking sound from the hatch behind him, followed by the hiss of the hatch seals. The hatch swung open and a dark-haired man in a blue jumpsuit appeared. Major Vladimir Kuzmin said in a thick Russian accent, "I thought I'd find you here, Tom."

Commander Wrye nodded toward Mars. "I wanted one last look before we launch."

"Ah," the Russian cosmonaut said. "You're thinking about the secret." He pushed off from the hatchway and floated toward the window.

"That's right," Commander Wrye said. "Lately, that's all I ever think about."

"I know," Major Kuzmin said somberly. "It's a heavy burden, knowing we shall soon launch for Mars—and when we get there, we will unlock a mystery that could destroy thousands of years of human science, culture, and religion."

Commander Wrye nodded slowly. "But we have a mission to carry out," he said, "and we'd better get to it. We launch in two hours."

With that, Commander Wrye and Major Kuzmin moved weightlessly toward the hatch—and toward an uncertain destiny.

At that same moment, two hundred fifty miles straight down from the International Space Station, a very different drama was under way in a place called Merkel's Department Store. In a glassed-in booth overlooking the main floor, the store's owner, Henry Merkel, sat beside the manager, Harvey Weems, watching an array of video monitors.

"That's him! That's Toby Brubaker!" the owner said. Mr. Merkel was a balding man with steely eyes like ball bearings, a nose like a hatchet, and a chin like a concrete block. "Zoom in on him! Get this on tape!"

"Right, Mr. Merkel," the manager said. Mr. Weems was a thin man with thin lips, a thin black tie, and thinning black hair.

"Oh, he's a slick one, that Brubaker boy," Mr. Merkel said, rubbing his hands together. "He's always sneaking in here, robbing me blind! This time, he's not getting away with it! Phone the police, Weems! I'm going downstairs to nab him!"

"Right, Mr. Merkel," Weems said.

Down on the floor of the department store, Toby Brubaker made his way through the electronics department, past displays of computers, scanners, TVs, VCRs, DVD players, stereos, camcorders, and digital cameras. As Toby walked down the aisle, his pale green eyes shifted right and left, continuously watching for Old Man Merkel. He knew Merkel was keeping an eye out for him—but for Toby, the risk of getting caught was half the fun of stealing.

Toby wore a bulky, dark green jacket—and not just because it was cold outside. He had opened up the inside lining, giving him secret pockets where he could stash stolen goods. He didn't realize a dozen security cameras were hidden throughout the store, capturing his bristly, close-cropped haircut, pasty skin, and pug nose on videotape.

Toby's jacket rattled with music CDs, an MP3 player, a personal CD player, and a Nintendo Game Boy. His eyes lit up when he saw a stack of video-game cartridges on a counter. After a quick check in all directions, he grabbed a handful of titles—*Weredragons III: Worlds of Extinction, Gladiator of Armageddon, Attila's Quest, Kickboxer Mania, Bushido Warriors*—and slipped them into his jacket. He did some quick mental arithmetic, then congratulated himself: His take so far was a little more than $450 worth of cool stuff! He was just reaching for a second handful when—

"Got you!" A bony hand clamped down on Toby's wrist. Toby looked up into the steely eyes of Henry Merkel.

"Dude!" Toby shrieked. "Where did you come from? Let go of me!"

"Not a chance, boy!" Mr. Merkel said. "The police are on their way—and you're coming with me!"

"Police!" Toby wailed. "Dude, don't call the police!"

Mr. Merkel gripped Toby's wrist with the strength of a vise, dragging the boy down the aisle. "Save your breath!" Mr. Merkel said. "We've got it all on videotape—proof that you've been stealing from my store!"

It was Allie O'Dell's first trip in her dad's new convertible—a red Jaguar XKR—and she wasn't enjoying the ride.

Red-haired and freckled, Allie usually wore a sparkling "tin grin," thanks to the braces that wired her teeth, but she didn't feel like smiling at the moment. Since her parents' divorce, Allie only saw her father every other weekend— and during those times, all he did was talk on the phone. *If I ever meet the guy who invented cellular phones*, Allie told herself bitterly, *I'm going to wring his neck!*

"Pete?" Allie's dad said into a slab of black plastic. He was lean and tanned with sandy red hair and rugged good looks. "Roger O'Dell, returning your call. I checked out that stock you were asking about. My advice? Dump it! The company's overweight and the stock is overvalued. They haven't made deep enough cuts in head count and fab utilization. Did you get my e-mail on that IPO? Well, that's where I'd put my money, if I were you. Hey, don't mention it, Pete. Later."

"Dad? Could you put the top up?" Allie asked. The wind had made a shambles of her carrot-red hair, blowing it all over her face and even into her mouth. *I could also wring the neck of the guy who invented convertibles!*

"Just a minute, kid," Allie's dad said, punching the buttons of his phone. "Got another call to make."

"But it's cold and the wind is blowing my—"

"Hey, Chuckie!" Allie's dad said. "Roger O'Dell here! Yeah, I was looking at your portfolio, and if I were you, I'd try for at least twenty percent from the long-term core position. The uptrends are still intact, so my advice is to hang on for the ride, set your sell-stops to preserve profits and your buy-stops to grab the next rally. Hey, no prob, Chuck. Later."

"Dad?" Allie said, peering through the windshield. "Why are you turning here?"

"Lunch," Allie's dad said. "I thought you were hungry."

"But this is the drive-through at Megaburgers!" Allie said. "You promised to take me *out* to lunch!"

"We're *out*, right?" Mr. O'Dell said. "And I'm buying you *lunch*, right? So I'm taking you *out* to *lunch*."

"You said we'd have lunch at Le Petit Bistro. You promised."

Mr. O'Dell shrugged. "You've always loved Megaburgers."

"Yeah," Allie said, "when I was in *elementary* school! But I'm in middle school now and I want a Monte Cristo sandwich at Le Petit Bistro."

"Monte Cristo sandwich?" Allie's dad asked. "That's just a ham sandwich soaked in grease! You don't want to eat all that fat, do you?"

"Oh, right!" Allie said. "I suppose a Megaburger is a fat-free health food!"

But Allie's father wasn't listening. He pulled the car up to the speaker and leaned over the door. "We want two Megaburgers, two orders of Megafries, and two chocolate Megashakes."

Allie folded her arms and sulked. "You promised we'd go to—"

"It'll save time to eat here," Mr. O'Dell interrupted.

"Could you at least turn off the cell phone?" Allie asked. "Could we talk?"

"Look, kid," her dad said, visibly annoyed, "I'm a busy man, and I need my phone to—"

"Please don't call me 'kid' anymore," Allie said. "You're always treating me like a kid and I'm not a—"

"Hold that thought," Mr. O'Dell said, raising his hand. He turned to the drive-through window and handed the clerk some cash. The clerk handed him a white paper bag with grease spots on the bottom, which he held out to Allie. She glared at him, arms folded, refusing to touch the bag.

Mr. O'Dell's jaw muscles worked back and forth. He jerked the red Jag convertible forward and flung the bag of fast food into a trash can.

"Look," Mr. O'Dell said angrily, "if you don't want Megaburgers, fine! We'll go to La Whatchamacallit and I'll buy you whatever you want—"

Allie gritted her teeth. "Grrrr! Don't you get it, Dad? I don't care about the food!"

"Then what—"

"I just want you to keep your promises," Allie said. "Is that so hard?"

Mr. O'Dell stared blankly at his daughter.

Allie rolled her eyes. "Oh, why waste my breath?" she said. "You promised to stay married to my mother—but you couldn't keep that promise, either."

Without speaking, Roger O'Dell angrily pulled his Jaguar convertible onto the street and roared away.

"Coming through!" Mr. Merkel called. "Make way!"

Startled customers parted as Mr. Merkel dragged Toby

along the main aisle of the department store. Toby's frightened eyes searched desperately for some way of escape.

"Dude!" Toby wailed. "Just let me go and I'll never come in this stinking store again!"

"It's too late for that!" Mr. Merkel said.

Toby saw the glassed-in booth up ahead, past the escalators, beyond the shoe department. Once Mr. Merkel got him in that booth, Toby would be trapped until the police arrived.

Toby glanced at the escalators. He saw a plump woman with an armload of packages coming down from the second floor. He had an idea: *If I time it just right . . .*

The package-laden woman stepped off the escalator directly in the path of Mr. Merkel and Toby. She had so many packages in her arms that she didn't see them. Toby grinned. *Excellent!*

"Excuse us, Mrs. Purvis!" Mr. Merkel called out to the package lady.

Mrs. Purvis tried to move to one side.

"Not that way, Mrs. Purvis!" Toby shouted. "The other way!"

Her packages leaning dangerously, Mrs. Purvis weaved back the other way—right into Mr. Merkel.

"Ooof!" Mr. Merkel said, losing his grip on Toby.

"Yowoooo!" Mrs. Purvis shrieked. Packages flying, she went down on the floor in an extremely undignified manner.

Toby dashed for the escalator. He leaped onto the moving stairs, taking two steps at a time—then he realized he was running up the down escalator! Though he was running up faster than the stairs were moving down, it was going to take him a long time to reach the second floor—and he had no time to waste.

Glancing over his shoulder, Toby saw Mr. Merkel jump to his feet and race to the escalator. Instead of following Toby up the down escalator, the store owner ran up the up escalator. Toby laughed—then turned and let the down escalator carry him back to the main floor. Reaching the foot of the escalator, he jumped off and zoomed around a group of people who were helping Mrs. Purvis to her feet.

"Come back here, Brubaker!" Mr. Merkel shouted from the top of the escalator. "You won't get away with this! I know where you live!"

Leaping over Mrs. Purvis's scattered packages, Toby dashed for the exit. As he reached the door, an alarm buzzed angrily. *Dude!* he thought. *When did Old Man Merkel start putting electronic security tags on his merchandise?* Not that it mattered. Merkel had already caught Toby shoplifting. There was only one thing for Toby to do: escape!

Outside the store, Toby sprinted across the parking lot. His thick jacket rattled as he ran—plastic CD cases clattering against plastic video-game cartridges and other stolen goods. Toby had escaped—but what now?

Old Hatchet Nose was right. Toby was in plenty of trouble with the law—and at home. The last time Toby had been caught stealing, his dad had smacked him in the face with the back of his hand. "That's just a taste of what you'll get," Toby's father had said, "if you ever get in trouble with the law again!" Toby had no doubt that he was in for a good thrashing this time.

Toby sprinted to the end of the block—and stopped in his tracks when he saw a police car coming around the corner. His heart thudded against his rib cage. Were the police looking for him? The car sped past him and turned into Merkel's parking lot. *Dude,* he thought. *I got away just in time! Those are the cops Old Hatchet Nose called!*

Toby's steps quickened.

Where can I hide? And then it came to him—the perfect place, a place no one would think to look for him.

2

THE FLYING GETAWAY CAR

The crew of the top-secret Mars mission had gathered in the Destiny Lab for a final prelaunch briefing. "There's not much left to say," Commander Wrye said, gripping a bulkhead handhold to steady himself in midair. "We all know our mission."

He paused and looked around at the five crew members who would be going with him to the Red Planet. In the front of the group was Major Vladimir Kuzmin, a veteran pilot who had flown many missions in the Russian *Soyuz* spacecraft. Next to him was Payload Specialist Hana Yamada, an expert in life-support systems; she was from Japan and was assigned to the Japanese Experiment Module (JEM). Behind her was Mission Specialist Lia Medina; she was a biologist from Brazil. Floating next to her was Mission Specialist Gerard Vachon, the noted French-Canadian archaeologist who had made many important discoveries among the Pyramids of Egypt and the ancient Mayan ruins in Mexico. Next to him was Mission Specialist Elsa Niemann, a language specialist from the European Union.

"The six of us will be the first human beings on Mars," Commander Wrye continued, "but our names won't go into the history books alongside the name of Neil Armstrong, the first man to walk on the Moon. There will be no live TV broadcasts, no news coverage, no speeches of 'one small step for man.' But even though this mission to Mars is a *secret* mission, every member of this crew is performing a great service to the human race. It's a privilege to serve with you all."

He paused and took a moment to look into the eyes of each crew member. Then he said, "All right—let's go to Mars."

Commander Wrye floated aside and let his crew make their way past him through the Destiny Lab. They floated through Unity Node, then climbed down through Node Three and entered Spaceship *Thuvia* through the ship's dorsal air lock. As the crew members disappeared below, Commander Wrye paused for a final look at the space station that had been his home for the past three months. He had grown to love this cramped, uncomfortable collection of can-shaped modules and wing-shaped solar panels. Even after three months, he still needed to read the yellow signs on the gray aluminum bulkheads to find his way around. Even so, he had come to think of the ISS as "home."

Well, he thought, *it's time to leave "home" and see what's waiting for us on Mars.*

With a sense of duty, destiny, and even a foreboding of doom, the American commander followed his crew into the belly of Spaceship *Thuvia.*

"Look, Allie," Roger O'Dell said after a long, tense silence, "I'm sorry I made you mad, okay?" He slowed the Jaguar for a stoplight. "I mean, you're right. I promised to take you to Le Thingamabob, and I shouldn't have broken my promise. Where is this place?"

Allie shrugged. "We don't have to go there. I'm not hungry anymore."

"No, really," her dad said. "I want to take you there. Where is it?"

"The Riverglenn Mall," Allie said. "Near the Super Cineplex."

"Okay, that's not far," Allie's dad said. The light turned green and Mr. O'Dell eased the Jaguar forward. "Fact is," he continued, "I've got some news to tell you—"

Allie looked sharply at her dad. "Good news or bad?"

"Well, I think it's good," he said. "I hope you'll think so, too."

"Uh-oh," Allie said softly. "What is it?"

"Penelope and I are getting married," he said, looking straight ahead.

Allie gasped.

"The company offered me a transfer," he continued. "Fortunately, it's in the same city where Penelope wants to settle down—close to her family and all."

"I see," Allie said. "You're leaving *your* family to be closer to *her* family."

"It's only three states away," he added. "It's not really that far—by plane."

"Just three states away, huh?" Allie said. "And when does this happen?"

"Oh, not for several weeks," her father said. "We'll get married and move in early December."

"I see," Allie said with an edge of bitterness. "And this is your 'good news'?"

"Well," her dad said, "it's good for Penelope and me. I was hoping you'd be happy for us."

"What about Christmas, Dad?" Allie asked.

"Christmas?" Roger O'Dell tugged at his collar as if it choked him.

"You won't be here for Christmas?" Allie asked accusingly.

"Hey, don't worry," he said. "I'll have some really neat presents sent over to you, and maybe we can get together for Easter. And you can come stay with us for a couple of weeks in the summer. How does that sound?"

"Peachy." Allie rolled her eyes. "Well, if this is your idea of good news, Dad, I'm glad you didn't have any bad news. Tell you what, let's skip lunch, okay?"

"Huh?" Mr. O'Dell looked surprised. "Why?"

"I'm not hungry. Take me over to Max McCrane's house, okay?"

"Max McCrane? Isn't he the guy with the—"

"Yeah, Dad," Allie said. "The guy with the time machine. He lives in that big Victorian house on Mirabilis Way."

"Okay, Allie," Mr. O'Dell said, checking his mirror and making a quick U-turn. "But you're not being very fair to me. I know this divorce business has been hard on you, but it's been hard on me, too."

"Oh, really? Divorcing Mom was your idea. I'm sure it must be perfectly awful for you, getting back into the whole dating thing, having a girlfriend again—especially when your girlfriend is that airhead, Penny Lope," Allie said sarcastically.

"Her name," he said, "is Penelope. You pronounce it Puh-NELL-O-Pea."

"Pronounce it any way you want to," Allie said. "Remember, she's the one who accused me of stealing her purse—then she found it right where she dropped it beside the sofa and never even apologized. So don't expect me to feel any warm fuzzies for her."

"Now, just a doggone—"

Allie angrily interrupted. "You divorced my mother, and now you're going to marry a woman I can't stand and move three states away. Oh, and to top everything off, you're not even going to be here for Christmas. Am I missing anything?"

"Well, you make it sound so terrible—"

"And not only do you give me all this wonderful news today, but you also want me to be *happy* for you!" Allie choked, and she quickly brushed her eyes with her fingertips.

"Okay, Dad, I'm happy, I'm ecstatic, I'm deliriously over-joyed. Now, please drive me to Max's house and let me out of this car!"

Roger O'Dell scowled. "You could at least show a little respect for your father."

Allie wanted to snap back, *You could at least show a little love for your daughter*—but she bit her lip instead.

They drove on in silence for several minutes. Finally, as they approached the end of Mirabilis Way, Allie saw Max McCrane's three-story Victorian house up ahead—

Then something alongside the road caught her eye: It was Toby Brubaker, dressed in a bulky green jacket, walking on the sidewalk in the direction of Max's house. *Strange,* Allie thought. *Toby doesn't live near here. . . .*

But as Roger O'Dell pulled the Jag in front of Max's house, Allie forgot all about Toby. All she could think of was her dad's awful "good news"—and how she wished she could go someplace millions of miles away.

Toby Brubaker looked up and saw a red Jaguar drive past and pull up in front of Max McCrane's house. *Dude!* he thought. *Can't let anyone see me!*

Up ahead was the grove of walnut trees that surrounded the McCrane property. He dashed for the shade of the walnut grove and hid himself behind a tree, peering out toward the front yard. A man got out of the driver's side of the Jag, and a red-haired girl got out of the passenger side. Toby frowned. *Miss Holier-Than-Everybody, Allie O'Dell!*

Then Toby saw the look on Allie's face. *Whoa!* Toby thought. *She looks mad!* Toby strained to hear what her dad was saying—

"Look, Allie," Mr. O'Dell said, "I don't want you to be mad. Isn't there something I can say—"

"No, Dad!" Allie snapped back. "Nothing! I just want you to leave me alone!"

Toby's eyes widened in surprise. *Whoa! O'Dell is yelling out her dad! Cool! Maybe she's not the Little Miss Goody-Goody she pretends to be!* Chuckling to himself, Toby stepped back behind the tree and waited as Allie and her dad walked toward the McCranes' front door.

As Allie rang the doorbell, Toby decided to sneak around to the backyard. Keeping in the shade of the walnut grove, he moved toward the rear of the house, wincing every time twigs and dry leaves snapped beneath his shoes. Reaching the backyard, he heard two familiar voices.

Peering around a tree trunk, he saw Max McCrane and Grady Stubblefield in the middle of the lawn beside a beat-up old Volkswagen Beetle. Toby strained to listen to their conversation.

Grady Stubblefield leaned against the dented fender of the old orange VW. He was a lean, athletic African-American with short hair and a broad grin. "Okay, Max," he said. "Where's this new invention of yours?"

"You're leaning on it," Max said, nodding to the car he called Timebender. Max McCrane had brown hair and brown eyes—eyes that were magnified behind the thick, round lenses of his eyeglasses. He stood with his hands jammed in his pockets.

"Come on," Grady said. "That's not a new invention! That's Timebender!" Max, Grady, Allie O'Dell, and Toby Brubaker had taken three previous trips in Timebender, an orange Volkswagen that Max had converted into a time machine.

"It's not the same old Timebender," Max said. "I've added something new—something that doesn't have anything to do with time travel."

"No way!" Grady said. "You're getting out of the time-travel business?"

"Fact is," Max said, "time travel makes me nervous. We've already taken three trips in time—and every time-trip we've taken has gotten us into trouble. I decided to invent something safer, something that wouldn't get us eaten by dinosaurs or stomped on by mammoths or tossed into a dungeon by some crazy old wizard."

"Yeah?" Grady said. "So what did you come up with?"

Max grinned. "Antigravity."

"Antigravity!" Grady scratched his head. "Doesn't sound so safe to me!"

"Well, I've already tested my antigravity machine," Max said, "and so far, I haven't hurt anybody or destroyed anything—so I figure it's pretty safe. I'll show you how it works." He reached through the broken driver's-side window and pulled out something that looked like—

"A video-game controller?" Grady asked.

"Sure," Max said. "This controller is from my old Nintendo. I spliced an extra-long cable to it, so I can control the car from the outside as well as the inside. Now, stand back and prepare to be amazed."

Max held down the red firing button, then thumbed the X/Y "joystick" controller. Without a sound, the car rose three feet off the ground.

Grady's eyes widened. "Whoa!" he said.

"Now, watch this," Max said. He nudged the joystick and the car started forward at about two miles an hour. The cable on the game controller went taut and the car started to swing in a slow, wide circle around Max. As the cable swung his way, Grady easily hopped over it.

Max carefully manipulated the game controller, bringing Timebender in for a gentle landing just inches from where it had lifted off.

Max chuckled. "Is that cool or what?"

"That," Grady said, "is way cool."

Something beeped in Max's hip pocket. He pulled out a yellow walkie-talkie and said, "Mom?"

"Your friend Allie is here," his mother's voice crackled. "And she has her father with her."

"Okay, Mom," Max said. "Be right there." Max stuck the walkie-talkie back in his pocket.

"What's that?" Grady asked. "Another invention?"

"Nah," Max said. "My mom bought a set of these at Merkel's Department Store. She was getting tired of hunting me down. Come on. Allie'll freak when she sees Timebender fly."

Max put the game controller back in the car, then he and Grady took off around the side of the house.

After they left, an intruder crept out of the walnut grove beside the backyard. The intruder had pale green eyes and a dark green jacket. He was running away from his parents, the police, and a hatchet-nosed man named Merkel.

"Dude!" Toby Brubaker said as he approached the ugly orange Volkswagen. "That dork McCrane finally came up with something I can use—a flying getaway car!"

Max and Grady found Allie and her dad on the front porch. "Hey, Allie!" Max called.

"Hi, Max," Allie said listlessly.

Max was startled. This was not the cheery Allie he knew so well. Something was definitely wrong.

Allie's dad approached Max and Grady, putting out his hand. "Hi, guys," he said, "I'm Roger O'Dell—Allie's dad."

Max shook his hand. "I'm Max McCrane," he said.

"Grady Stubblefield," Grady said, shaking the man's hand.

Standing next to her dad, Allie rolled her eyes.

"Allie's told me a lot about you fellas," Mr. O'Dell said

with an amused smile. "She says you've all traveled together in a"—he chuckled—"a time machine?"

"That's right," Max said. "It's in the backyard, if you want to see it."

"Come on," Mr. O'Dell said. "It's a gag, right? I mean, aren't you guys a little old for 'Let's Pretend'?"

"It's not pretend," Grady said. "It's a real time machine."

Mr. O'Dell gave the boys a doubtful look—but they both seemed completely serious. "Okay," he said. "Let's see this time machine of yours."

Allie scowled. "I thought you were in a hurry," she said bitterly.

Mr. O'Dell grinned. "I can spare a few minutes," he said, "to see a real time machine."

"Right this way," said Max, leading the way to the back-yard.

Toby reached through the broken window and pulled out the game controller. A glowing yellow light on the con-troller told him the power was on. *How does this thing work?* he wondered. He pressed the red firing button. Nothing happened. He pushed the joystick. Nothing hap-pened. He held down the firing button and pressed the joy-stick at the same time—

The car jumped three feet in the air!

Toby was so startled that he pressed the joystick the other way.

The car slammed onto the grass, bouncing on its bald tires.

Toby turned to see if anyone had seen him—and he heard approaching voices. *Dude!* he thought. *They're coming! Where can I hide?* There was no time to run back to the walnut grove. Looking around, he could see only one place to hide. . . .

Max, Grady, Allie, and Mr. O'Dell walked up to the beat-up old Volkswagen. Mr. O'Dell peered in through the broken windows.

"It's in pretty bad shape," Max said.

Mr. O'Dell laughed. "It looks like it's been in a demolition derby, all right," he said. "But to me, this car is a thing of beauty."

Max blinked behind his round glasses. "You're kidding."

"I used to own one of these old Beetles when I was a college student," Mr. O'Dell said. "It was neon green, made you sick to your stomach to look at it, and I loved that old car. I wish I'd never sold it."

Max laughed. "I saw that red Jaguar convertible you drive. What would you want with an old VW Beetle?"

"Sure, I've got a Jag," Allie's dad said. "But looking at this orange wreck of yours really takes me back to the good old days."

"Show him what this 'orange wreck' can do," Grady said.

"I'm sure my dad is way too busy to—" Allie began.

"Well, I would like to just sit in it for a minute," Mr. O'Dell said.

"Tell you what," Max said. "Get in and I'll fly you around the backyard."

Mr. O'Dell grinned, disbelieving. "Fly?" he said. "First, you tell me this car is a time machine—and now you're telling me it can fly?"

"Max, stop kidding," Allie said. "Timebender doesn't fly!"

"Allie, this is something new!" Grady said. "Max invented an antigravity machine! Wait till you see it."

Allie looked doubtful. "An antigravity machine?"

"Okay," Mr. O'Dell said, smirking. "Let's take a spin in your flying car."

"Cool," Max said. "Okay, Grady and Allie in the backseat, and Mr. O'Dell, you're up front with me."

They piled into the Volkswagen. "Mr. O'Dell," Max said, "would you hand me that pocket calculator in the glove box? Thanks." Max punched some numbers into the handheld calculator. "The car weighs eighteen hundred pounds," he said. "Now I need the weight of everybody in the car—if you're off a couple of pounds, that's okay, but we need to have a pretty close estimate. Mr. O'Dell?"

"Okay," Mr. O'Dell said. "I'll play along. I'm a hundred and seventy-eight pounds."

"Allie?"

"That question is so rude," Allie said, "but if you must know, I weigh ninety-nine pounds."

"A hundred and eight," Grady said.

"And I'm a hundred and two," Max said, punching in the last of the numbers. "I know this seems weird, but I need everybody's weight so I can feed the right amount of power to the repulsor."

"Oh, right," Mr. O'Dell said. "The repulsor. Nice touch. Very sci-fi."

Max picked up a computer keyboard from between the seats and tapped the number keypad. A display screen, duct-taped to the dashboard, lit up with numbers. He picked up the game controller. "Here goes," he said. He pressed the red firing button, then pushed the joystick forward, and—

Nothing happened.

"Whee," Mr. O'Dell said sarcastically. "We're flying."

"Something's wrong!" Max said. "It worked fine a few minutes ago. Maybe I made a mistake in the calculations—"

"Or maybe somebody lied about her weight," Grady said, nudging Allie.

"Don't look at me," Allie said.

"Maybe it would help if we flapped our arms," Mr. O'Dell said, chuckling. "Well, it's been fun, but I need to—"

"Let me try it one more time," Max said. "Mr. O'Dell, would you put this keyboard on the floor by your feet? I want to recheck these numbers."

Mr. O'Dell took the keyboard—but as he held it, his thumb pressed down on the "+" key. Nobody in the car noticed the numbers on the dashboard display were changing— fast. The numbers went higher and higher until Mr. O'Dell set the keyboard down and took his thumb off the "+" key.

Max tapped on his handheld calculator, then said, "Hmm. The calculations check out, but the antigravity doesn't work—almost as if the car's too heavy."

"Maybe you've got a stowaway on board," Mr. O'Dell said.

"Max McCrane!"

Max looked out the broken window. His mom stood on the back porch of the house. She was a thin woman with brown hair, a lined face, and worried-looking eyes.

"What is it, Mom?" Max called.

"Aren't you forgetting something?" she called.

"Aw, Mom!" Max said, wincing.

"You are not to leave this property until your room is cleaned up!" his mother said. She came down the steps and walked out to the middle of the lawn.

"I won't leave the property, Mom," Max said. "I'm just—"

Mr. O'Dell's cellular phone made a shrill chirping sound—*deedle-deedle-dee!* He took the phone from his pocket and flipped it open. "Roger O'Dell speaking," he said. "Oh, hi, Phil. Sure, I have a few minutes. I'm just sitting in a flying time machine, waiting for takeoff. Ha-ha! I'll tell you about it later—"

"And remember what your father said," Max's mother added. "You are not to leave our space-time whatcha-macallit without permission."

"Our space-time continuum?" Max said. "I know."

"I wouldn't touch that stock right now, Phil," Mr. O'Dell said into his phone. "The company's suffering from a broadband glut and too much third-party debt. I'd wait until the sector attrition has shaken out the market, then take another look."

"Mom," Max said, "I'm only going to take the car three feet off the ground."

Max's mom wrung her hands. "I don't know, Max. Maybe your father should look at that car first. What if you hooked up the wrong wires or something?"

"Don't worry, Mom," Max said. "Nothing could possibly go wrong. Watch." He pressed the red firing button on the game controller, then pushed the joystick forward—

And the car shot into the sky.

A thunderclap knocked Max's mother onto the grass— the sound of a Volkswagen breaking the sound barrier. Flat on her back, Mrs. McCrane watched the VW Beetle vanish into the sky.

Then she jumped up and ran toward the house, screaming for her husband. "Oswald! Oswald, come out here quick! Max has done it again!"

3

FACES IN THE STARS

Commander Wrye was sitting in the command chair, going through his prelaunch checklist, when a voice crackled over the radio. "Space Station Launch Control to *Thuvia*," said the Control voice. "We've got a UFO on long-range scan. It lifted off from North America, and it's moving this way—fast."

Commander Wrye flipped some toggle switches on his control panel, then checked the main video screen. A blip moved swiftly across the green screen. "I have it on my scanner," he said. He shot a worried glance at Major Kuzmin, who was strapped in to the copilot's seat on the right. "It's moving at—that's impossible! Nothing could move that fast through the atmosphere without burning up!"

"It's on a collision course with ISS," said the Control voice. "It will traverse our orbit in . . . five seconds." Collision alarms blared throughout the spaceship.

Five seconds, thought Commander Wrye. *Whatever that thing is, it's either going to vaporize us or miss us by an eyelash.*

"Three seconds," said Major Kuzmin. "Two . . . one . . ."

Something shot past the forward viewpanes of Spaceship *Thuvia.* Commander Wrye and Major Kuzmin both saw it—something orange and rounded, but moving so fast it was hard to get a good look at it. It had missed Spaceship *Thuvia* and the ISS by about a hundred yards, maybe less. And the shape of the thing—

If Commander Wrye didn't know better, he would have sworn it was shaped like a Volkswagen Beetle.

With saucerlike eyes, Roger O'Dell looked through the windshield, where the blue sky swiftly darkened to a black void sprinkled with stars. Something whooshed past— something made of big metal cylinders and flat solar panels. Mr. O'Dell looked at the hissing cellular phone in his hand. "I was in the middle of a call," he said numbly. "I got cut off when we—but that's impossible! We couldn't be—"

"Flying?" Max said, sitting behind the steering wheel. "I'm afraid we are, Mr. O'Dell. In fact, I think that was the International Space Station we passed back there."

"Max!" Allie said. "Max, take us back!"

"Yeah!" Grady said. "We're, like, in outer space or something!"

In the seat next to Max, Mr. O'Dell turned pale. He

gripped the passenger seat with both hands to keep from floating. "Outer space? We can't be! Volkswagens don't fly in outer space!"

"This one can!" Allie said breathlessly, rising off the car seat. Her hair floated as if she were under water. "Max, look!" She pointed out the rear window of the Volkswagen.

Max checked the rearview mirror and saw the blue-white marble called planet Earth shrinking in the distance behind them. "This is bad," he said. "If that was the space station, then we must have traveled two hundred fifty miles straight up in about ten seconds! That's twenty-five miles a second!"

"Max!" Allie said. "Stop this car! Get us back on the ground this instant!"

Max turned and looked at Allie. "I can't," he said sorrowfully.

"What do you mean, you can't?" Grady said, putting his hands against the car roof to keep from drifting into the air. "You've got to!"

"You guys don't understand," Max said. "We're traveling at about ninety thousand miles an hour—that's almost four times faster than escape velocity!"

"Escape velocity?" Allie asked. "What's that?"

"Escape velocity is the speed at which you need to launch an object off the surface of Earth so it won't fall down again. Do you understand what I'm saying? We're leaving Earth, and we can't get back."

"That's silly!" Allie said. "Just make a U-turn and go back the way you came!"

"I can't," Max said. "Timebender is an antigravity machine. It can push itself away from Earth's gravity, but it can't pull itself back again. The thing I don't understand is—Oh, no!"

"What?" Grady said, floating forward from the backseat.

Max pointed to the dashboard display. It was lit up with nines all the way across. "The power input is set to maximum! No wonder we're traveling at impossible speeds. How in the world—" Max stopped and looked at Mr. O'Dell.

"Oh!" the man said. "When you handed me the keyboard, I must have—"

"Dad!" Allie moaned. "How could you do that?"

"It's not his fault, Allie," Max said. "It's mine. I should have double-checked the dashboard display before liftoff."

"This can't be happening," Mr. O'Dell groaned.

"Max," Allie said. "I don't get it. We're in outer space, the windows of the car are broken—How are we able to breathe?"

"I'm not sure," Max said. "But I think the antigravity field creates a discontinuity—an invisible layer of force separating Timebender from surrounding space. That discontinuity keeps our air from leaking out—and it also kept the air from Earth's atmosphere from burning us up like a meteor. It might also explain why we weren't smashed into a puddle of goo when we took off from the surface of the earth at ninety thousand miles an hour. The antigravity field must cancel out inertia."

"Inertia?" Allie asked. "What's that?"

"The tendency of an object to resist motion," Max said. "Like when you're in a roller coaster that accelerates real fast—inertia pushes you back in your seat. Timebender's antigravity field must also act as an anti-inertia field."

"So," Allie said, "the antigravity field is keeping us alive."

"Yeah—for now," Max said. "But we're using up the air inside the car. Eventually, we won't be able to breathe in here."

"How long before the air runs out?" Grady asked.

"You won't like the answer," Max said. "My guess is that in about half an hour, we'll be—" He couldn't bring himself to finish his sentence.

But then, he didn't have to.

Spaceship *Thuvia* was a cylinder of titanium steel as long as twenty school buses, packed with tons of scientific equipment and more than a thousand miles of electrical wiring. Constructed of metal, polymers, carbon fiber, ceramics, and quartz, powered by a high-thrust nuclear thermal engine system, *Thuvia* was the most complex machine ever built by human beings. Assembled in orbit by the International Space Authority, the ship was a hive of equipment panels, electronics boxes, cables, hydraulics, coolant tubes, bulkheads, struts, payload bays, air locks, solar arrays, and computer terminals.

Now *Thuvia*'s mission was in doubt. The near miss by the mysterious UFO had thrown the entire International Space Authority into an uproar. Space officials from a dozen countries asked: What did the sudden appearance of the UFO mean? Was it an attack? Was it a message? Perhaps the UFO's near approach to the ISS was a warning: *Do not launch the mission to Mars—or the next time we won't miss.* But if it was a message, who sent it? The UFO hadn't come from space—it had come from Earth. In fact, it had launched from within the United States!

What did it all mean?

Aboard Spaceship *Thuvia*, Commander Wrye and his crew were strapped into their acceleration chairs, ready for a launch that might never happen. The countdown was on hold. The suspense was unbearable. Finally, a voice crackled over the radio—and six astronauts almost jumped out of their skins. "Launch Control to *Thuvia*," said the voice.

"Wrye here," said the commander. "What's the word, Control?"

"The International Space Authority has reviewed the UFO incident," said the voice of Launch Control. "Here are the orders: 'Mars mission more urgent than ever. *Thuvia* to proceed as planned. Prepare to launch.'"

Archaeologist Gerard Vachon and Language Specialist Elsa Niemann cheered. Commander Wrye and Major Kuzmin high-fived. Hana Yamada and Lia Medina grinned and gave the thumbs-up sign.

Commander Wrye spoke into his throat mike. "That's great news, Control."

"Have you been informed of the UFO's heading?" the Control voice asked.

"I assumed it was headed out of the solar system," Commander Wrye said.

"Negative," the Control voice said. "It's on an intercept course for Mars."

"Mars!" Commander Wrye cast an astonished glance at his Russian copilot.

The Control voice continued, "Space Authority thinks the UFO may be connected with the secret on Mars. You thought you had one mystery to solve. Now, it appears you have two."

"Is it just me," Allie asked, "or is it getting cold?" She floated over the backseat, her body doubled up, her wire-covered teeth chattering.

"It's not just you," Max said. "It's definitely getting colder."

"And harder to breathe," Grady said.

Grady was right. Max was straining for each breath. He reached into his pocket and felt his asthma inhaler there— but he didn't take it out. The problem wasn't asthma. The problem was too much carbon dioxide and not enough oxygen. Soon the breathable air would be gone—and it would all be over.

"God," Grady prayed aloud, "You've gotten us out of impossible jams before—but this one looks like the worst one yet. Please save us—"

"No!" Allie said, gasping. "I don't want to hear any prayers!"

Max turned around so quickly, he bumped his head against the roof. "Allie!" he said. "How can you say that?"

"Look!" Allie said, her eyes full of tears, "God doesn't care about us! If He did, we wouldn't be in this mess!"

"Come on, Allie!" Max said. "This isn't His fault."

"I don't believe it, Allie," Grady said in a wounded voice. "You're the one who always trusted God, no matter how bad things got."

"Yeah?" Allie said, shivering and gasping. "Well, I'm sorry I can't live up to your expectations, but it's been a really bad day. First, I found out my dad is getting married and moving away, and now I'm going to die in space. Excuse me for being grouchy!"

"Allie," Mr. O'Dell said, his voice choking, "I know I haven't been the best father in the world, but I want you to know—"

"Look, Dad," Allie interrupted, "it's a little late to go mushy on me now." She shut her eyes tightly, squeezing out tears that floated on the air.

Max checked the rearview mirror and saw that Earth and the Moon were very distant, very small. All around the car were millions of stars. Up ahead, one star glowed more brightly than the rest—but it was not actually a star. It was a planet, and it was red.

"Mars!" Max whispered through chattering teeth.

"What's that, Max?" Grady gasped.

"Mars," Max said. "Mars." He was getting sleepy. *Was this what happened when there wasn't enough oxygen in the air?* Max looked around.

Mr. O'Dell floated with his face turned toward Allie. His eyes looked tormented. Allie floated behind him, gasping for every breath. *Was she crying? Asleep?* Max couldn't tell.

Max looked at Grady, and Grady gave him a thumbs-up sign and a brave half-smile. "Are you sure, Max?" Grady asked through trembling lips. "Are you sure we can't go home?"

"I'm sure," Max said. "I'm sorry."

"It's okay," Grady said. "I'm ready. Don't feel bad."

Max returned a shivery half-smile, then he closed his eyes and prayed. He prayed for Allie, Grady, and Mr. O'Dell. He prayed for his mom and dad, who would miss him. As he prayed, his thoughts began to jumble. It was cold, so cold. . . .

He opened his eyes and looked around. Allie and Grady seemed peacefully asleep as they floated in the back of the car. Next to Max, Mr. O'Dell hovered, his eyes closed, his sandy hair drifting on the air like seaweed in an ocean current.

Beyond the windows, millions of stars glowed softly. Then Max saw the faces.

I'm dreaming, Max told himself. *Or maybe I'm just seeing things.*

The faces seemed loving and caring, intelligent but not really human. The most surprising thing about these faces was the color—

Blue faces with golden eyes, Max told himself. *I'm definitely seeing things.*

Then Max's thoughts faded into the cold and darkness of space.

4

ROADWAY IN THE SKY

Maneuvering thrusters fired, pushing Spaceship *Thuvia* gently away from the massive structure of the International Space Station. Minutes ticked away in the cold silence of space, two hundred fifty miles above the surface of Earth. Soon, Spaceship *Thuvia* was a mile from the station, then five miles, ten, twenty, thirty . . .

Suddenly, the nuclear thermal engines flared to brilliant life. Spaceship *Thuvia* shot away on a blinding plume of white-hot energy. The top-secret mission had begun. Commander Thomas Wrye and his crew were on course for Mars.

Each member of the crew had spent a lot of time thinking about what they would find on the Red Planet. Not one of them imagined what actually awaited them there.

Max was the first to awaken. He had been dreaming about a bright, warm place. He opened his eyes and saw the top of the Volkswagen just inches from his nose. He stretched his arms—and they felt strangely stiff, as if he had been asleep for days.

Max looked around. Just beyond his reach, Grady floated in a curled-up position with a faint smile on his face. Allie was also sleeping. So was Mr. O'Dell.

Max took a closer look at Mr. O'Dell. The man had been clean-shaven before. Now, however, he had a sandy red beard to match his hair—at least two weeks' growth, maybe more. It didn't make sense.

Max pulled his weightless body downward behind the steering wheel. Peering through the cracked windshield, he saw something that looked like the Moon, only it was a dull red color. Then he remembered.

Mars! That's Mars up ahead—and we're all still alive. That, too, made no sense. The last thing Max remembered, they had been freezing to death and running out of air— and Mars had been millions of miles away.

Something streaked past the window—a bright flash of blue light, like a blue meteor. It shot ahead of Timebender, toward Mars, and disappeared in the distance—but it left behind a faint blue afterglow. Then came another streak of blue light. It, too, disappeared toward Mars, leaving a faint trail. Then came more streaks of blue light, and more, and more—they flashed past on both sides and underneath Timebender. The faint trails of light joined together, forming a path through space, a roadway of transparent blue radiance. It was as if Timebender was riding a highway of light that led straight to the Red Planet.

Max checked the dashboard displays—they were dark. *No power!* he thought. *But that's impossible! The only thing keeping us alive is the antigravity field! Without that, we'd lose our air and—Whoa! Our air!*

That's when it hit Max that he was breathing easily—no gasping for breath! They had been running out of air when he lost consciousness! Now, there was plenty of air. Again, it didn't make sense. Nothing made sense.

Then Max noticed a faint blue shimmer surrounding the car—so faint it was almost invisible. It flickered along the metal windowframes and glimmered across the hood and danced around the steering wheel. It looked like the same blue glow that the roadway in space was made of. *Was that pale glow keeping them alive?*

Then he remembered—the faces! Just before he had fallen asleep, Max had seen blue faces with golden eyes! He felt a tingle of fear—and excitement. Either something horrible was about to happen—or something wonderful.

"Max?" said a sleepy voice behind him—Allie's voice. "Where are we?"

Max turned and saw Allie looking at him. Her carrot-red hair floated like mermaid tresses. "Looks like we're going to Mars," Max said.

"Mars?" said another sleepy voice—Grady's. "Where's Mars?"

"Out there," Max said. "Dead ahead."

"Ooooh!" Mr. O'Dell groaned, squinching his eyes shut.

"Oh, man, are my muscles stiff! I dreamed I was in an old Volkswagen Beetle and we—" He opened his eyes. "Oh, no," he said. "It wasn't a dream."

"Dad!" Allie said. "You have a beard!"

Mr. O'Dell felt his chin—and his face paled. "How long have we been sleeping?"

Max checked his calendar watch. "Whoa!" he said. "We left Earth seventeen days ago! If I ever get home, I'm going to be *so* grounded!"

"Seventeen days!" Grady said. "No wonder I'm so hungry! Can you imagine what Toby would say if he was here? That guy is *always* hungry."

Looking out the windshield, the four travelers saw Mars growing steadily larger in front of them. The rust-colored surface was blotched with patches of gray and black, and spattered with craters.

"We're coming in over the southern half of Mars," Max said. "I recognize some of the features. Up ahead is the Hellas Impact Basin—the lowest point on Mars."

"How do you know so much about Mars?" Mr. O'Dell asked.

"He's a science whiz, Dad," Allie said. "He knows more about Mars than you know about the New York Stock Exchange. Right, Max?"

Max reddened. It was embarrassing when people made a big deal about how smart he was. "Well," he said, "I guess you could say that Mars is kind of a hobby of mine."

"Look at those craters!" Grady said. "Zillions of them!"

"Why is it so dark up ahead?" Allie asked.

"We're passing into the nightside of the planet," Max said.

Mr. O'Dell looked at Max, then at Allie and Grady. "You guys seem so calm!" he said. "I mean, we've crossed millions of miles of empty space—in a Volkswagen Beetle! And that's Mars out there! This is not only dangerous—it's impossible! But the three of you act like you've done this before!"

"I tried to tell you, Dad," Allie said. "We have."

"Allie!" Mr. O'Dell said. "You mean, those stories you told me about being chased by a dinosaur, and seeing a dragon, and—"

"All true," Max said.

"I don't know why you didn't believe me, Dad," Allie said.

Minutes passed. The roadway of blue light took them through the nightside of Mars and brought them into the Martian dawn. As the VW descended toward the planet, the feeling of weight returned, and they settled into their seats.

"The blue road is taking us to the surface," Allie said. "What happens to us then? In science class, Miss Hinkle told us that human beings can't live on the surface of Mars."

"That's right," Max said. "The average temperature on Mars is around eighty degrees below zero. Even if it wasn't so cold, breathing would still be a problem. The air on Mars is a hundred times thinner than the air on Earth, and it's over ninety-five percent carbon dioxide and less than one-tenth of one percent oxygen."

"We'll die down there!" Mr. O'Dell said, his voice rising.

"I don't think so," Max said calmly. "This blue highway in space didn't just appear by accident. Someone kept us alive this far—and I think they've probably provided life support for us on Mars. If not"—he shrugged—"it's been a short, interesting life, and I'll see you guys in heaven."

They flew on in silence for a couple of minutes.

Allie pointed ahead. "What is that?" Something vast and dark loomed up on the horizon—a huge, broad mountain. It squatted on the rusty-red face of Mars like an immense scab.

"That's Olympus Mons—or Mount Olympus," Max said. "See those craters on top? It's the largest volcano in the solar system—a hundred times bigger than the biggest volcano on Earth. Olympus Mons is about as wide as the state of Arizona, and three times higher than Mount Everest."

The roadway of blue light tilted steeply downward. As the Volkswagen nosed more sharply toward the Martian surface, Max, Allie, Grady, and Mr. O'Dell felt a dizzying sensation as if they were on a roller-coaster ride.

"Whoa!" Grady said. "Cool!"

"It looks like we're angling north," Max said, checking the position of the morning sun of Mars.

"What's that dark blotchy place up ahead?" Allie asked. "It goes all across the horizon."

"I'm not sure," Max said. "It could be . . ." He paused— then he pounded the steering wheel in excitement. "Whoa! No way!"

"What?" Allie said.

"What's wrong?" Mr. O'Dell asked in alarm.

"Nothing's wrong!" Max said. "In fact, if we're headed where I think we are, this is going to be the coolest trip we've ever made!"

They continued descending through the Martian sky.

"Look at the blue road!" Allie said, pointing. "It's bringing us in for a landing."

Up ahead, the blue road made a downward spiral to the left over a smooth plain dotted with flat-topped mesas and pyramid-shaped mountains.

"It's true!" Max said. "This is it!"

"This is what?" asked Mr. O'Dell, his voice shaking.

"Look there!" Max said. "See that cluster of five pyramids in a grouping like a five-pointed star? That's called the Pyramid City. Notice how all the pyramids in this area seem to have five sides. And see that formation that looks like a huge castle? It's called the Fortress. And look over there, beyond the Fortress. Recognize that?"

Allie, Grady, and Mr. O'Dell looked where Max pointed—and they all saw it at once: the Face on Mars.

"Guys," Max said, "welcome to Cydonia."

The other passengers were silent and in awe. They had all heard of the Cydonia region and the Face on Mars. Allie had done a report on Cydonia in Miss Hinkle's science class. Grady had read a book titled *The Monuments of Mars,* then wrote a book report for his English class. Even Mr. O'Dell had heard of Cydonia—just days before, while in the dentist's office, he'd read a magazine article about it.

As Timebender descended, the four travelers could see

that the Face on Mars looked damaged, worn, and crumbled with age. Still, it obviously looked like a face. Sometime in the distant past, it had been carved by intelligent beings and left as a monument—but a monument to what? It looked like the face of an intelligent being, but it didn't exactly look human. Suddenly, Max realized what it reminded him of: the face of a *snake*.

The roadway of blue light made a sweeping turn around the Face, taking Timebender in a wide U-turn around the structure. The Face was incredibly huge—1.6 miles long, 1.2 miles wide, and a third of a mile high. The four faces at Mount Rushmore and the Sphinx in Egypt would have been mere dust motes next to the Face. The expression of the Face seemed cold and remote, arrogant and cruel, intelligent but reptilian. It wasn't hard to imagine it as the face of an alien king—or an alien god or demon.

"We're coming in for a landing," Max said. "Everybody hold on tight!" Looking out the windshield, the four travelers could see nothing but rust-red ground in front of them. It looked like they were going to crash.

Allie bit the back of her hand to keep from screaming. Mr. O'Dell and Grady grabbed the armrests and seats, bracing for impact. Only Max seemed unafraid. He was straining forward, gazing intently at the Martian landscape.

The ground rushed up—

The car leveled off—

And Timebender's four bald tires touched down in a smooth, featherlight landing. The entire trip had been so quiet that it was startling to hear the *shussss* of tires rolling across Martian sand, the creaking of old Volkswagen springs, the rattling of old car parts.

Up ahead was the Fortress. The walls of the Fortress rose steeply from the Martian desert, half a mile high. Those towering walls were covered with carvings of horrible reptilian creatures interwoven with strange scenes of warfare in space, zooming comets, bursting stars, and exploding planets. The centermost section of the main wall was dominated by massive double doors, over which was a carved replica of the Face on Mars—a humanlike/snakelike face. The carvings of the Fortress were worn by time and countless Martian sandstorms, but somehow the ancient Fortress still seemed inhabited and in use, not abandoned or forgotten.

The Volkswagen rolled straight toward the Fortress at about fifty miles an hour, and it showed no signs of slowing down. Max checked the power displays—they were still dark. The car couldn't be moving under its own power. Something was pulling Timebender along—but what?

Allie shrieked and pointed forward. The double doors of the Fortress were parting, sliding to either side. Three jetliners could have fit through the doorway, side by side, with room to spare.

The Volkswagen entered the shadow of the Fortress. As it rolled through that massive doorway, it was like a guppy swimming into the mouth of a whale. Once inside the Fortress, the Volkswagen rolled down a ramp and into a vast, oval-shaped depression that resembled a sports arena—like an indoor football stadium, only much larger. The arena was surrounded on three sides by rows of massive stone columns, all intricately carved. The VW gently slowed until it came to a stop in the middle of the arena.

"Look behind us!" Allie said, pointing out the rear window of the car. Everyone looked. The huge double doors were sliding closed, shutting out the pale Martian sunlight. Max, Allie, Grady, and Mr. O'Dell were trapped inside the Fortress.

The doors thudded shut—but the interior of the Fortress was not completely dark. Beyond the rows of carved stone columns were rows of massive machines. The machines appeared to be made of massive blocks of stone, huge bands and rods of metal, and gigantic balls of crystal. Weird energies of purple and red crackled within those crystalline spheres, casting shifting shadows around the arena.

For a long time, no one spoke.

"Okay," Grady said at last. "What happens now?"

5

THE FORTRESS OF EVIL

Spaceship *Thuvia* was seventeen days into its journey to Mars. Mission Specialist Lia Medina tethered herself to her computer station, using a cord clipped to the belt of her jumpsuit. The cord enabled her to work at the computer without floating away. Commander Wrye floated next to her, grasping a handhold that jutted from the bulkhead.

"This is the long-range scan we just received from the Space Station," Lia said, her English flavored with a trace of Brazilian Portuguese.

The commander pointed to a moving blip on the screen. "That's the UFO?" he asked.

Lia nodded. "The Space Station trackers watched it all the way. It didn't even accelerate—it just shot away from Earth at about forty kilometers per second, and maintained that speed all the way to Mars."

Commander Wrye whistled. "That's over ninety thousand miles an hour. It shot off Earth as if gravity had no effect on it."

"It took us two weeks of steady acceleration to reach half that speed," Lia Medina said. "With the time it takes to accelerate and decelerate, it's going to take us fifty-nine days to reach Mars. The UFO made the trip in seventeen days."

"When will it land?" Thomas Wrye asked.

"It already landed," she said, "or crashed. It went down in the northern hemisphere, in the Cydonia region."

"Cydonia!" the commander said. "*Our* destination. Well, I think there's no longer any doubt about it. Whatever that UFO is, it has some connection with our mission—and with the mystery on Mars."

Max, Grady, Allie, and Mr. O'Dell waited inside the Fortress, not daring to move from the car. They looked around the arena and beyond, searching for moving forms—human or alien—lurking behind the stone columns or among the red-glowing crystal-sphere machines. They saw no one.

"Okay," Max said, "where's the welcoming committee?"

"I don't think anybody's home," Grady said. "Want to get out and look around?"

Beep-beep-beep!

Max jumped and looked to his right. Mr. O'Dell sat next to him, punching buttons on his cellular phone.

"Dad," Allie said from the backseat, "what are you doing?"

"I'm calling nine-one-one!" the man said nervously. "Nobody's answering!"

"Well, duh!" Allie groaned. "Dad, the nearest cellular tower is, like, zillions of miles from here."

"Actually," Max said, "it's about thirty-eight million—"

"Besides," Allie said, "even if you reached nine-one-one, what should they do? Send out a space shuttle?"

Mr. O'Dell looked annoyed—and a little embarrassed. "Okay, okay, it was a dumb idea. But I haven't heard any other ideas for getting us out of this fix." He peered anxiously out the car's broken windows. "And since I'm the only adult here, it looks like I'm in charge—"

Allie groaned. "Oh, Dad, puh-leeeze! If you want to help, just stay out of the—"

"Allie!" Grady said softly, leaning close to her ear. "Your dad's just trying to be helpful—and you've been treating him really mean."

Allie stared at Grady with shocked eyes. "Mean? Me? What about the way he—"

"Look," Grady whispered, "I know you're mad at him, but that doesn't give you the right to be sarcastic and disrespectful. He *is* your dad, you know."

"But you don't know how he—," Allie sputtered.

Whatever she was about to say was interrupted by a shout from Max. "Hello!" Max called, leaning out the broken window.

"Is somebody out there?" Mr. O'Dell asked, nervously glancing at the flickering shadows all around them.

"I don't see anybody," Max said. "I just thought if I called out—"

"Hello!" said a rumbling, echoing voice.

Everyone jumped. Allie gave a sharp scream.

A faint blue glow appeared all around them. Out of the glow, figures emerged—humanlike, but not human, glowing with a soft blue light. At first, Max and the others noticed only a few glowing beings. But soon there were dozens, then hundreds, then *thousands* of them. Their eyes gave off a soft, golden radiance. The beings surrounded the Volkswagen on every side, crowding the interior of the Fortress like a great assembled army.

Hands shaking, Max opened the door and stepped out of the car. He turned all around and stared in awe at the thousands of blue glowing faces that gazed back at him. Grady, Mr. O'Dell, and Allie followed him and looked around, trembling.

One of the blue beings stepped forward. "My name is Zaykiel," he said, "and I am pleased to welcome five travelers from Earth."

"*Five* travelers?" Max asked, glancing at his friends. "There are just four of us!"

Thump! All four travelers jumped at the sound from under the hood of the Volkswagen. *Thump! Thump! Thump!* "McCraaaaaaane!" shouted a muffled voice. "Let me out of here, you dork! I'm suffocating!"

"Oh, no!" Allie groaned.

Max grabbed the latch and raised the hood of the car. Curled up in the luggage compartment was Toby Brubaker, clad in a heavy green jacket. "Don't just stand there, McCrane!" Toby said. "Help me out of here! My legs are so stiff I can hardly move!"

Max helped Toby climb over the front bumper. There was a clatter of hard plastic somewhere inside Toby's jacket as he clambered out of the car. Toby stood up, looked around—and saw thousands of glowing blue beings with golden eyes.

"Dude!" Toby groaned. "I hate when this happens! Where are we this time?"

"We're on Mars," Allie said.

"Mars!" Toby said. "I hate Mars! McCrane, why can't this stupid car of yours ever take us someplace really cool? And who are all those glow-in-the-dark guys?"

"We," said Zaykiel, "are the Timelings—Emissaries of Elyon and guardians of this solar system."

"Elyon?" Mr. O'Dell asked. "Who's that?"

"Elyon," Zaykiel said, "is one of the names of the Most High God." The Timeling turned his golden gaze upon Max. "It is a special honor to meet you, Max McCrane."

Max blinked behind his round glasses. "You—you know who I am?"

"Of course," the Timeling said. "You are a hero of the Battle Before Time. Throughout Elyon's Realm, the story is told of how you invented this wonderful machine"—he pointed to Timebender—"and how you and your friends journeyed to the edge of Creation and back. Oh, yes, we know you, and we honor you—Max McCrane, Bender of Time."

An awed murmur went through the vast crowd of blue-glowing Timelings. Thousands of blue-glowing heads bowed in respect.

"I—I—" Max stammered bashfully. "I don't know what to say."

"And you, Allie O'Dell and Grady Stubblefield," the Timeling said, "are also well known to us. Along with your friend Max, you faced the Enemy and defeated him by your obedience to Elyon the Most High, and by your faith in His Son. The tale of your victory over the Dragon of Eden has been told and retold many times in Elyon's Golden Realm."

"What about me?" Toby said. "I was there, too, you know."

"Yes," the Timeling said. The glow in his golden eyes dimmed. "Your part in the story is also well known to us, Toby Brubaker. Your story is unfinished, your future is clouded. Indeed, that is why you were brought here."

"A lot you know!" Toby sneered. "Nobody brought me here. I just happened to be hiding in McCrane's dorky car, and he must've pushed the wrong button or something. I came here totally by accident."

"In the Eternal Plan," the Timeling said, "there are no accidents."

"Wait a minute!" Max said, pounding his fist against his palm. "It just hit me! Toby stowed away and messed up my weight calculations! If he hadn't done that, we wouldn't be in this mess!"

"Oh, right!" Toby said. "Blame me when your stupid car goes haywire!"

"It doesn't matter whose fault it is that we're here," Grady said. "I think Zaykiel is telling us that even things that *seem* accidental are all part of Elyon's Plan."

"Wisely said," Zaykiel replied. "It has been written that all things work together for good to those who love Elyon and are called to serve His Eternal Plan. Every human life is a story—a drama played out upon the stage of time and eternity. When you see your life as a story, you understand your place in the mind of the Most High."

"Look," Mr. O'Dell cut in, his voice rising, his jaw muscles working. "I don't know who you people are or what you want with us, but I demand that you take us back to Earth right now! I'm an American taxpayer, and I know my rights!"

"Please remain calm, Roger O'Dell," the Timeling said. "I understand that you are confused and afraid, but I assure you—"

"Me? Afraid?" Mr. O'Dell said. "Ha-ha!" He intended his laugh to sound bold and confident, but it ended up as more of a frightened giggle.

"It's okay, Mr. O'Dell," Grady said. "We're all scared. This is the fourth crazy trip I've taken with Max, and I *never* get used to it."

"We Timelings are here to help you," Zaykiel continued, "especially you, Toby Brubaker—"

"Drop dead," Toby sneered.

"—and you, Allie O'Dell," Zaykiel finished, turning his golden gaze in her direction.

Allie folded her arms, glaring. "I don't need any help," she said.

"Allie O'Dell," Zaykiel said, taking a step toward her, "Elyon has told us that your heart has been deeply wounded. There is much anger inside you—and much hurt."

"My feelings," Allie said, "are none of your business!"

"Allie!" Grady whispered, nudging her. "The Timelings want to help us. Don't be that way!"

Allie rolled her eyes and turned away.

"Zaykiel," Max said, "you say you are called Timelings?"

"Yes," Zaykiel said, "we Timelings are a special class of Emissaries. We have been commissioned by Elyon to enforce his verdict against the Enemy and the Dark Emissaries. Elyon has granted us authority over time and space in this solar system."

"When we were in space," Max said, "running out of air to breathe, I saw you—just before I blacked out."

"Yes," Zaykiel said. "We placed you in a state of deep sleep, replenished your air, then brought you here to Mars."

"About this place you brought us to," Max said. "Our scientists call it 'Cydonia.' Who built these buildings? Who carved the Face?"

"This is your second visit to Mars, correct?" Zaykiel asked.

Max nodded.

"The first time you were here," Zaykiel said, "you met

the Enemy, the Evil One. This place you call Cydonia was his stronghold."

"And the Face?" Max asked.

"It was an image of the Evil One himself," Zaykiel said. "He ordered the other Fallen Emissaries to carve it as a monument to his power and arrogance."

"And this building we are in right now?" Max asked. "Our scientists call it the 'Fortress.'"

"Your scientists have named it well," Zaykiel said. "Before the Enemy was banished from Mars, this structure was his Fortress of Evil."

"What's going to happen to us now?" Grady asked.

"Each of you has been brought here for a purpose," Zaykiel replied. "That purpose will soon be revealed."

A strange, deep sound rolled across the Fortress—a sound like the heavy rumble of planets rolling in their orbits, the awesome thunder of fiery suns, the ponderous wheeling of galaxies through endless time and barren space.

"What's that sound?" Max asked—but the moment he asked, he knew that the sound came from the Timelings themselves. It was a chorus of thousands of Timeling voices, swelling in a strange, soul-deep song that was both beautiful and terrible.

"The time has come," Zaykiel said.

Allie looked shaken and afraid. "The time for what?" she asked.

"The time of testing and growing," Zaykiel replied in a gentle voice. "The time of learning and healing." Zaykiel turned and faced the thousands of blue Emissaries who crowded the arena of the Fortress. "Ariyel," he called in a loud voice. "Jarael."

Two Timelings stepped forth.

"Toby Brubaker," Zaykiel said, "you will go with Ariyel. Allie O'Dell, you and your father will go with Jarael. Max McCrane and Grady Stubblefield, you will come with me."

"But we don't want to be separated," Allie said.

The Timeling named Jarael stepped up to her and took her hand. "Come," Jarael said. The crowd of Timelings parted, and Jarael led Allie and her father off toward one corner of the vast Fortress. As she was led away, Allie cast a reluctant glance over her shoulder, toward Max and Grady.

The other Timeling, the one named Ariyel, turned to Toby. There was a gentle expression on the Timeling's face. Though the Timelings never exactly smiled, Ariyel's golden eyes radiated mercy—even pity. "Toby Brubaker," Ariyel said in a friendly voice. "You will come with me."

Toby shook his head. "Uh-uh, nope, no way. I'm staying right here."

Ariyel's voice never changed, nor did the look in his eyes—yet something about him seemed forceful and commanding as he repeated, "You will come with me."

"All right!" Toby said. "Dude! You don't have to be so mean!" He followed the Timeling toward a different corner of the Fortress.

The deep, mournful chorus of the Timelings swelled—
then faded to an echo.

Zaykiel turned to Max and Grady. "Pray for your friend
Allie and her father," the Timeling said. "And pray for
Toby. Pray for yourselves, too. Much depends on what
happens in the next few hours."

6

A World Ripped in Half

Spaceship *Thuvia* sailed through space at a cruising speed of twenty kilometers per second, or just under forty-five thousand miles per hour.

Commander Wrye swam through the crew compartment, floating to the command chair. Major Vladimir Kuzmin was strapped into the right-hand seat, peering out at the stars through the forward viewpanes, sipping a bulb of coffee.

"What's the latest on our UFO?" the Russian asked.

"It landed on Mars," Commander Wrye said.

"Near Cydonia?" Major Kuzmin asked.

Commander Wrye blinked. "How did you know?"

"I have been thinking about that UFO," Major Kuzmin said. "It launched from Earth at the same time we were preparing to launch from ISS. It flew right in front of our noses. Its destination? The same as our destination—Mars.

We'll be landing at Cydonia, so where else should the UFO land but Cydonia? Too many coincidences, my friend. Our mission and the flight of that UFO are connected—it's all part of some plan."

"I agree," Commander Wrye said. "But *whose* plan?"

Allie and her father walked along beside the Timeling, Jarael. They passed the towering stone columns and approached the massive machines of stone, metal, and clear crystal. Red energies throbbed in the crystal spheres. *Destructive energies,* Allie thought. *I wonder what the power generated by these machines might have been used for—*

And then she remembered the war in space she had seen on their first adventure in time. She had seen blasts of frightening power attacking the forces of Elyon—energies that had probably come from these very machines.

"I don't even know why I'm going along with this nonsense," Mr. O'Dell muttered, stroking his beard as they walked. Then he turned to the Timeling in annoyance. "You know," he said, "my daughter and I haven't had a bite to eat in seventeen days."

"Food will be provided," Jarael said.

They came to a wall with a series of archways. The wall was ornamented with carvings of hideous creatures, including dragons and serpents. Allie glanced at the carvings, then looked away, shuddering.

Jarael selected one of the archways and led them into a darkened tunnel. Allie and her father stayed close to Jarael. The gloom in the tunnel was so deep, so dark, it clung to their skin like a black film. The only light in the tunnel was the Timeling's strange blue glow.

"So, what do Timelings do?" Mr. O'Dell asked as they walked. "I mean, isn't it kind of boring, just standing around in this Fortress with nothing to do?"

"You are mistaken, Mr. O'Dell," Jarael said. "We don't live here. In fact, this is the first time I've been to Mars in many centuries. Elyon called us to Mars because we were needed here."

"Really?" Allie said. "Then where do you live?"

"I am usually assigned to Earth," Jarael said. "A very troubled place, Earth. The Enemy is very busy there. But it is also a fascinating world, one of Elyon's most beautiful creations."

"What do you do on Earth?" Allie asked.

"I help people," Jarael said. "Sometimes I protect people from evil and harm. Sometimes I help people learn the things Elyon desires to teach them. And when I'm not busy, I enjoy reading books."

"Really?" Allie said, surprised. "You read books? Books written by human authors?"

"Why are you surprised?" Jarael said. "You like to read books, don't you?"

"Sure, I do," Allie said. "But—"

"And so do I," Jarael said. "Amazing invention, books. I was there when Emily Dickinson wrote some of her most beautiful poems. I watched Mark Twain at work as he penned some of his best novels. I was even there when Shakespeare wrote some of his wonderful plays. You can pick up a book, and those authors—even though they have been dead for years or even centuries—can still speak to you from the pages of a book."

"Cool," Allie said. "I never thought of books that way before."

"Jarael," Allie's father said, "I suppose you've read the Bible, haven't you?"

"Of course, Mr. O'Dell," Jarael said. "I know it by heart, from cover to cover, in every language ever written."

"That figures," Mr. O'Dell said. "Anyway, Allie's always quoting the Bible to me and telling me I should do what the Bible says."

"That would be my advice, also," Jarael said.

"Well," Mr. O'Dell said, "doesn't the Bible also say something about how kids should respect their parents?"

Allie glared at her father. "Maybe if you'd set an example I could respect—"

"Allie," Jarael said sharply. "You know that God wants you to honor your father, even if you don't agree with him."

"But that's not fair!" Allie said. "*He's* the one who's wrong, not me!"

"At the moment," Jarael said, "I don't see either of you living according to the will of Elyon."

Allie was about to argue—but she figured it was hopeless trying to argue with one of Elyon's Emissaries.

Scowling, she folded her arms and walked on in silence. Minutes passed. They continued on through the dark tunnel, nobody speaking.

Then Allie looked up and gasped. "Stars!" she said, stopping in her tracks.

Mr. O'Dell stopped and looked up. "Hey! You're right. When did we come out of the tunnel? I was sure we were moving deeper underground."

"We were," Allie said. "I know we were. And it was broad daylight when we entered the Fortress. It couldn't have gotten dark that fast."

Mr. O'Dell turned to the Timeling. "Where are we?"

"I know where we are," Allie said. "We're on Earth."

"Earth!" Mr. O'Dell said, disbelieving. But as he looked around, he knew Allie was right. There were shadowy trees all around, black shapes against a star-frosted sky. There was no moon, but the stars shed a faint light. They were on a tree-lined ridge, and down below them, at the foot of the slope, was a lake.

"I smell campfire smoke," Allie said.

"Yeah," Mr. O'Dell said, sniffing the air. "So do I."

Allie breathed in the green scent of pine and fir. "I know this place," she said. "This is Clear Lake! We used to come here when I was little. But we haven't been here since—" She stopped abruptly, leaving the rest of her thought unspoken.

"Come," Jarael said. The Timeling led them around some granite outcroppings, past a stand of fragrant balsam firs, and into a clearing. There was a campfire in the middle of the clearing, a bright Coleman lantern, and a big red ice chest.

Mr. O'Dell turned to Jarael and said, "Where did you get that stuff? That's my camping gear!"

"In the ice chest," Jarael said, "you'll find food and drink."

Mr. O'Dell went to the ice chest and looked inside. He found bottled water, hot dogs, buns, mustard, catsup, relish, and paper plates. Beside the ice chest were a couple of long sticks, sharpened for use as hot dog skewers. "Looks like someone thought of everything." He looked up at Allie. "You want a hot dog?"

Allie shrugged.

Mr. O'Dell frowned. "I'll take that as a yes," he said. He proceeded to skewer two hot dogs. He handed a dog-on-a-stick to Allie; she took it without a word of thanks and crouched beside the campfire, holding the hot dog over the flames. Mr. O'Dell sat down on a log beside the campfire and roasted a hot dog for himself.

A minute of awkward silence passed.

"Hey, kid," Mr. O'Dell said. "Oops, sorry. I mean, Allie—are you still mad?"

Allie shot him a hostile glare. "What do you think?"

Mr. O'Dell nodded and looked away. Another minute passed in silence. Mr. O'Dell uncapped a couple of water bottles, handed one to Allie, and sipped from the other. "Ahh, that's good," he said, wiping his mouth with his sleeve. "There's something about space travel that makes a guy thirsty."

"Ha-ha," Allie said sarcastically.

"Hey, I'm just trying to make conversation," Mr. O'Dell said.

Another minute passed. The hot dogs began to sizzle. A meaty, spicy aroma filled the air. Mr. O'Dell glanced at Jarael, who stood on the far side of the fire. "Is this what you had in mind? For Allie and me to roast hot dogs and not talk to each other?"

"What would you like to say to your daughter?" Jarael asked.

Mr. O'Dell scowled. "Never mind," he said. He leaned the stick on a rock next to the fire, so that the hot dog stayed close to the heat. Then he put hot dog buns on two plates and passed one to Allie. In silence, Allie and her dad applied mustard, catsup, and relish, then began eating.

"Mmm," Mr. O'Dell said. "Good hot dogs."

"Yeah," Allie said. "Tastes just like the hot dogs we had the last time we—" She stopped and let the sentence dangle.

"The last time you camped at Clear Lake?" Jarael asked.

Allie turned to her dad. "That was the happiest day of my life. You and Mom had been fighting a lot for, like, six months or so. But then you said, 'Let's go camping at the lake,' and we had that one perfect weekend together. And you and Mom didn't fight once all weekend. I thought, *Yes! Everything's going to be okay!* But a few nights later—"

"Do we have to talk about this?" her father interrupted.

"She has to talk," Jarael said, "and you have to listen."

"A few nights later," Allie continued, "you told me that

you and Mom were getting a divorce. And I said, 'Why? We had such a great time at Clear Lake! Why can't we just go on like that?' And you said you were only acting nice to each other so that I could have one nice family weekend before it was over."

Crouching beside the fire, Allie looked down at the half-eaten hot dog in her hands. She wasn't hungry anymore. She stood and tossed the rest of the hot dog into the fire. "Thanks a lot, Dad," she said. "Thanks for the nice fake smiles and fake happiness and fake togetherness. Now, every time I think of Clear Lake, I think, *That was the weekend before I lost my family.*"

"What are you so mad about?" her father said with his mouth full. "You haven't had such a bad life. I make good money and give you lots of nice things."

"Yeah," Allie said. "You gave me a nice, big, empty house to live in. You gave me my own TV and my own computer and my own bed with a pillow to cry on."

"Oh, get off it, Allie!" her father snapped. "You're such a drama queen!"

Allie looked stricken. "Drama queen? You think this is an act?"

"Okay," he said, "I shouldn't have said that. But I've talked to experts on child psychology, and they tell me that kids are resilient. Sure, divorce hurts for a while, but you'll get over it."

Allie's eyes shone wetly in the firelight. "Right, Dad," Allie said. "Just because my whole world is ripped in half is no reason to be upset."

Her father rolled his eyes. "Oh, brother."

"Go ahead, Dad," Allie said. "Write it off. There goes Allie O'Dell, the Drama Queen, making a big deal out of nothing!"

Mr. O'Dell glowered at Allie. "Look, kid—Allie," he said, "I'm sorry about the divorce. Maybe this whole thing has been harder on you than I realized. But what am I supposed to do? Stay married to your mom even though we can't get along anymore?"

"That's what you promised to do," Allie said. "I watched the video of your wedding the other day, and I cried all the way through it. I heard you promise to love Mom 'for better, for worse, till death do us part.'"

"I know what I promised," her father said, "but I didn't know how hard it would be to keep that promise."

"Maybe you just didn't try hard enough," Allie said.

Mr. O'Dell started to reply—then he stopped himself. What could he say? Allie was right.

7

THE VALLEY OF THE SHADOW OF DEATH

Commander Wrye checked the control panel. All of Spaceship *Thuvia*'s systems were normal. He looked out of the forward viewpane. The bright light that was Mars shone red before them, threatening and mysterious.

Thomas Wrye turned to Vladimir Kuzmin. "Vladi," he said, "do you believe in God?"

"I hardly ever think about God," the Russian said with a shrug. "In Communist Russia, I was taught that God is a fairy tale. My greatest hero was Yuri Gagarin, our first cosmonaut. When he came back from space, he said that he had proved there is no God, because he had gone into space and had not seen God there."

Commander Wrye shook his head. "What did Gagarin expect to see? An old man in a long white beard sitting on a throne in outer space?"

Kuzmin shrugged, grinning. "And you? Do you believe in God?"

Wrye was silent for a long time. "I did once," he said. "Not anymore."

"Oh?"

"My faith in God was burned out of me when I was attending the university," the commander said. "I was taking a course in astrophysics. The first day of class, Professor Selkirk stood up in front of the class with a Bible in his hands. He opened it to Genesis 1 and read: 'In the beginning, God created the heavens and the earth . . .' He read the whole chapter to us—then he tossed the Bible into a trash can and said, 'Now, I'm going to tell you the truth!' That year, I learned all about stars and galaxies, black holes and wormholes, dark matter and antimatter. Professor Selkirk often said, 'You don't need God to explain the universe.'"

"So this Professor Selkirk destroyed your faith?" Major Kuzmin asked.

"Not right away," Commander Wrye said. "I clung to my faith for a while. One time, I tried to debate Professor Selkirk. I went to him and said, 'For every effect, there must be a cause, correct? So what caused the universe to exist?' He said, 'Ah, you think that, since the universe exists, God must be the cause.' I said, 'Of course.' He said, 'Fine, let's say God caused the universe. Now, I have a question for you: What caused God?'"

"What did you say?" the Russian asked.

"I had no answer," Commander Wrye said. "That was when I realized that my faith in God had begun to collapse."

Max and Grady got up from their knees. The memory of Zaykiel's words echoed in their minds: *Pray for your friend Allie and her father. And pray for Toby. Pray for yourselves, too. Much depends on what happens in the next few hours.*

"Hey!" Grady said, looking around the arena of the Fortress. "Where did all the other Timelings go?"

Max looked around. He and Grady were alone with Zaykiel.

"My fellow Timelings left while you were praying," Zaykiel said. "They have returned to their duties throughout the solar system."

"What happens now?" Grady asked.

"Are you hungry?" Zaykiel said. "If so, take this and eat." The Timeling held out something in both hands. It looked like pieces of golden cake.

"What is it?" Max asked.

"Taste," Zaykiel said, "and see."

Grady and Max looked at each other; then they each took a piece and ate it. The cakelike stuff was firm to touch, but melted on the tongue. It was sweet, with a honeylike flavor—but not *too* sweet. Just a few bites satisfied both their hunger and thirst.

"I have some things to show you," Zaykiel said, "but first, Max McCrane, I would like you to show me something."

"What's that?" Max asked.

"Your antigravity machine," the Timeling said.

"Really?" Max said. "Okay." He led Zaykiel and Grady around to the rear of the car and opened the engine cover.

"Ah!" Zaykiel said. "This is the repulsor, correct?" The Timeling pointed to a spindle that held what appeared to be a compact disk coated with a dull gray substance. The disk was held in a horizontal position, and was ringed by a series of electromagnets—bars of black iron wrapped with insulated copper wire.

Max nodded. "My aunt Agnes gave me a Britney Spears CD for my birthday, and I figured I might as well get some use out of it, so I coated it with an electronics-grade ceramic and used it as a repulsor."

Zaykiel leaned closer, examining a stainless-steel coupling that supported the spindle and disk. "And what is this?" he asked.

"That's a universal joint," Max said. "I bought it at an auto parts store and modified it. The joint tilts the spinning disk and—"

"And the angle of tilt," Zaykiel said, "changes the angle of gravity repulsion, so you can move forward, backward, or side to side."

"You're right!" Max said. "Hey, you must know a lot about machines."

"Well," the Timeling said, the golden glow in his eyes brightening, "matters of science and inventions are something of a specialty with me. Each of us Timelings has a special area of interest. Jarael, who is with your friend Allie, has a fascination with books, stories, plays, and poetry—the literature of the human race. And Ariyel, who is with your friend Toby, has spent many centuries study-ing human ambition, greed, and lust for power."

"Perfect!" Grady said. "Ariyel will get a good, close look at ambition and greed if he spends time with Toby."

"Why are the Timelings so interested in what human beings do?" Max asked.

"Each Timeling," Zaykiel said, "has a unique interest that enables him to carry out a special task in service to Elyon. For example, I am better able to understand you, Max, because we share an interest in machines, inventions, and scientific principles."

"Oh, I see," Max said. "And Jarael can relate to Allie and her love of books—and Ariyel understands why Toby acts the way he does. That's really cool."

"Yes," Zaykiel said. "The wisdom of the Most High is quite, um, 'cool.' Now, getting back to your antigravity device—" The Timeling turned back to the VW and pointed at something in the engine compartment. "This disk spins under the influence of the magnets, correct? And if I'm not mistaken, the magnets are powered by this device here." He pointed to a metal canister about the size of a fire extinguisher.

"Yeah," Max said. "There's a small amount of anti-matter in that canister, suspended in a magnetic field."

"Antimatter?" Grady said. "What's that?"

"It's like regular matter," Max said, "except that its atoms are made of antielectrons and antiprotons—particles with the opposite spin and charge from regular electrons and protons."

"Oh," Grady said. "Thanks for clearing that up."

"Antimatter," Zaykiel said, "is also extremely dangerous. A fraction of a gram, if released from that magnetic container, would cause an explosion greater than a nuclear bomb."

Grady's eyes got big. "Max! That car could go off like an atom bomb?"

"It's completely safe," Max said. "The magnetic container is stable as long as it has power. The antimatter provides an endless supply of power."

"Where did you get it?" Grady said.

Max shrugged. "My dad was using antimatter for a research project. He once told me I could borrow his laboratory stuff as long as he wasn't using it."

"And—," Zaykiel prompted.

Max bit his lip. "And as long as I asked permission. . . . I guess I forgot that part."

"You *forgot?*" Zaykiel said.

"Okay, okay," Max said. "I didn't forget. I just took it without asking." He looked away. "But I needed it! Antimatter's the only power source strong enough to run an antigravity machine."

"If you had asked permission," Zaykiel said, "would your father have said yes?"

Max shook his head. "No." He looked at Zaykiel. "Okay, you're right. When we get back to Earth—if we get back—I'll tell my dad about taking the antimatter. I can hear it now: 'You took antimatter without permission and went to Mars? You're grounded for life—again!'"

"I'm sure everything will turn out all right with your father," Zaykiel said. "Now, let's take Timebender for a tour of Mars, shall we?"

Max pointed to the VW. "Really? You want to ride in this?"

"I'd be honored," the Timeling said.

Max, Grady, and Zaykiel got into Timebender. Max noticed that a pale blue glow surrounded the car once more. Max did his calculations, allowing for the low gravity of Mars. Then they were ready to go.

Behind them, the massive double doors of the Fortress slid aside. The pale Martian sunlight streamed in. Taking the game controller in his hand, Max turned on the power, then lifted off. Timebender silently rose three feet off the floor. Max angled the repulsor and the Volkswagen sprang forward. He brought the car around in a nice, tight U-turn. Timebender soared out of the Fortress and into the Martian sky.

As Timebender ascended, Max turned to Zaykiel. "Which way?"

Zaykiel pointed to the right. "South."

Max knew what lay south of Cydonia. "Cool," he said, grinning. With a gentle touch of the joystick, he urged Timebender southward.

"Let's go higher," Zaykiel said. "I'll give your vehicle a boost in speed when we reach the upper altitudes."

Max increased power to the repulsor, and Timebender ascended. Grady punched the lock button of the car door.

Max grinned at him. "What's the matter, Grady? Don't like my driving?"

"I'm not too crazy about heights," Grady said.

The Martian sky was blue at higher altitudes—a deeper and darker blue than the skies of Earth. "Closer to the ground," Grady said, "the sky looks pink. Up here it's blue. Why is that?"

"The dust in the air makes the sky pink," Max said. "Up here, there's less dust."

"What makes the dust red?" Grady asked.

"Iron oxide in the soil," Max said.

"Iron oxide?" Grady said. "That's rust! You mean Mars is just—"

"Yep," Max said, grinning. "Just a big rust-ball in the sky."

The dark, smooth landscape below gave way to a rippled plain. The land appeared to have been shaped by flowing water, then pitted with meteor craters. "Down there somewhere," Max said, "is where the first Viking space probe landed in 1976."

As they flew farther south, the land became increasingly rough and crater-scarred. Some of the craters they saw were several hundred miles across. As they passed over a huge, winding canyon, Max said, "That's the Ganges Chasma." He pronounced it GAN-jees KAS-muh.

"Awesome!" Grady said, gazing into its depths.

"Yeah, it's awesome, all right," Max said. "But it's just a gopher hole compared to that canyon out there." He pointed toward the horizon.

Grady looked where Max pointed and saw a vast scar on the distant terrain, partially obscured by pink haze. It stretched across the rim of the planet from east to west.

"Begin your descent, Max," Zaykiel said. "Ease us down slowly."

Max gently decreased the power to the repulsor, and the Volkswagen began its long, slow glide toward the surface of Mars.

The Timeling leaned forward and pointed off toward the right. "Let's head a little more to the west, Max," he said. "There's something I want to show you there."

Max touched the joystick, angling the repulsor. The car made a gentle turn to the west. For the next twenty minutes, they descended in silence. The air around them grew thicker, hazier, and steadily more pink.

Ahead, the horizon-to-horizon scar in the ground grew closer. Its sides were horizontally striped with ribbons of different-colored rock.

"It's—it's a canyon," Grady said in an awed voice. "But it's so huge!"

"It's called Valles Marineris—the Mariner Valley," Max said. "It's three thousand miles long, over a hundred miles wide, and five miles deep. The Grand Canyon in Arizona is a scratch in the dirt compared to this."

"Keep descending," Zaykiel said. "We'll set down in that valley."

"I see it," Max said. He brought the Volkswagen in low over a mountain ridge. He eased off on the power and leveled the repulsor, slowing their forward motion. Then he gently settled the VW onto a smooth patch of rust-colored ground. They were down.

Max looked all around. "This place . . . looks . . . familiar," he said slowly.

"I remember this valley," Grady said. "This is where we met the Enemy."

Max's mouth dropped open. "Whoa! That's it! But it's so different!"

"The last time you were here," Zaykiel said, "was thousands of years ago."

For several moments, neither Max nor Grady could speak. Their minds were flooded with memories—vivid images from their first visit to the fourth planet from the Sun. Max, Grady, Allie, and Toby had arrived on Mars with their newfound friend, the golden Emissary, Gavriyel. The surface of the planet had been destroyed by the Enemy. Back then, the ground had been blackened and burning; now it was red and rocky. The once-jagged mountains were now smooth and worn down by time.

"Let's get out of the car," Zaykiel said.

Max looked alarmed. "What about the atmosphere? We'd die out there!"

"Max," Zaykiel said, "do you think this flimsy vehicle of yours protects you from the atmosphere out there? Come."

Max nodded, feeling a little foolish. He opened the door and stepped onto the Martian surface—and he noticed a faint field of blue light that clung to his skin. It was the same protective shield that had surrounded Timebender itself.

Zaykiel pointed down the valley slope to a place of deep ravines and shadows. "Let's go see the place where you met the Enemy," he said.

Max and Grady exchanged glances. The memory of that awful experience was still fresh in their minds.

"Come," Zaykiel repeated. Then he turned and started down the slope. Max and Grady followed.

The Timeling led them across crumbly, wind-swept ground, and into a deep notch between two rock walls. As Max and Grady followed Zaykiel into the narrow crevice, they remembered how Allie had recited softly as she walked, "Though I walk through the valley of the shadow of death, I will fear no evil, for You are with me. . . ."

The notch in the rocks opened out upon a wide ledge overlooking a deep canyon. Zaykiel, Max, and Grady came out onto the ledge. A natural stone bridge had once spanned the canyon, but had since collapsed. On the far side of the canyon, the mouths of several caves dotted the cliff wall. The largest cave, Max and Grady recalled, had been the last refuge of the Enemy before he was exiled to Earth.

"This is where we stood," Max said, "when we met the Enemy. When we were here the first time, I thought this canyon was huge. But I know it's just a narrow little gully that branches off the biggest canyon in the solar system."

Max pointed to the caves across the canyon. "Why was the Enemy holed up in those caves?" he asked.

"The forces of Elyon attacked the Enemy at his stronghold in the Fortress of Cydonia," Zaykiel replied. "So the Enemy and his Dark Emissaries were forced to retreat to this place. There are many caves here in the canyons of

Valles Marineris. This is where the Enemy chose to make his last stand on Mars, before he was exiled to Earth."

Max stared silently across the canyon, remembering how the Enemy had roared his defiance at Gavriyel, promising more death, more destruction, more war. The Enemy's defiance had baffled Max. *Hadn't Gavriyel and the rest of Elyon's Emissaries won the war? Wasn't the Enemy defeated? Wasn't the war over?* No, Gavriyel had said, the war wasn't over. In fact, the *real* war was just beginning—but the battlefield had shifted. From that moment, the battle would no longer be fought among the stars, but among human souls.

Max shivered as he remembered, though he didn't feel cold. In that instant, he realized why he and his friends had returned to Mars. The war between the eternal God and the ancient Enemy was raging in billions of human souls on Earth—and also in a handful of human souls, right here on Mars. That war was being fought in the souls of Max and Grady, in the souls of Allie and her dad, and in the soul of Toby Brubaker.

Max and Grady looked at each other and saw the truth in each other's eyes: The choices Allie, Mr. O'Dell, and Toby were making at that very moment were part of the ancient battle between the forces of God and the forces of the Enemy. Each choice had eternal significance. Instantly, Max and Grady knew what they had to do.

On that rocky ledge, overlooking the Martian canyon where they had first met the Enemy, Max and Grady dropped to their knees and began to pray.

8

ALONE IN THE DARK

Mission Specialist Lia Medina stared wide-eyed at her computer screen. The image on the screen was not merely absurd—it was impossible. "Commander Wrye," she called. "You'd better see this."

Commander Wrye unclipped himself from his command chair and swam through midair toward the back of the crew compartment. He floated up behind Lia Medina, grabbing a handhold to steady himself. The screen displayed a photo of the Martian surface taken by the Hubble Space Telescope. In the center of the photo was a man-made object.

Commander Wrye couldn't believe his eyes. "Is that the UFO?" he asked.

"ISS tracking confirms it," Lia Medina said.

"I don't believe it," Commander Wrye said. He turned and called to the rest of the crew. "Hey, everybody—look at this. Tell me if you see what I see."

Major Vladimir Kuzmin moved back from the copilot's chair. Mission Specialists Gerard Vachon and Elsa Niemann floated over from their computer terminals. Payload Specialist Hana Yamada moved in through the hatch from the payload bay. They all gathered around Lia Medina's computer screen. "What is it?" Hana Yamada asked.

"There's our UFO," Commander Wrye said, pointing to the screen. "It's sitting in a little valley north of Valles Marineris. What does it look like to you?"

In unison, almost as if it had been rehearsed, the crew of Spaceship *Thuvia* said, "A Volkswagen!"

Toby walked along behind the Timeling Ariyel through a gloomy tunnel. He put the last bite of honey-sweet cake-like stuff in his mouth and let it melt on his tongue.

"Hey, Blue Dude!" he said, licking his fingers. "That sweet stuff isn't bad. What is it?"

"You could not pronounce the name," Ariyel said.

"I don't care what you call it," Toby said. "You got any more?"

"You're not hungry, are you?" Ariyel said. "Or thirsty?"

Toby was surprised to realize he was not. "Hey," he said, "you're right. But I'd like to carry some in my pocket for later."

"If you become hungry later," the Timeling said, "food will be provided."

Ariyel glided effortlessly, silently through the shadows and gloom. Toby couldn't hear the Timeling's footsteps. He could only hear his own labored breathing and hurried footsteps as he struggled to keep up with the blue-glowing being.

"Dude!" Toby said. "Where are we going?"

Ariyel said, "You'll know soon enough."

"What's the hurry?" Toby asked. "Can't you slow up a little?"

"Come along," Ariyel replied.

Toby looked around him and saw strange, towering shadows in the gloom. He glanced to the left and right, and sometimes he thought he caught a glimpse of staring eyes or grasping claws among the deeper shadows. Was it just his imagination, or was the Fortress haunted?

"This whole trip is whack, man!" Toby grumbled as he struggled to keep pace. "I shouldn't even be here. It's all McCrane's fault—him and his dorky Timebender! He's always coming up with some stupid invention—and he practically gets me killed every time. Every place we go, we run into these freaky glow-in-the-dark guys! This is totally messed up! If I ever get off this stinking planet, I'll never—oooof!"

Toby tripped over some unseen crack in the floor and went flying in the dark. He landed on his stomach with the wind knocked out of him. For a few moments, he lay sprawled on the cold stone floor. Then he looked up and saw Ariyel ahead, walking off as if he hadn't noticed that Toby was no longer with him.

"Hey!" Toby wheezed. "Blue Dude! Come back here!"

But the Timeling didn't answer and didn't stop. He passed through an archway that led into a darkened corridor and was gone. Toby was alone.

Heart racing, Toby jumped to his feet and tried to follow Ariyel—but with the blue glow of the Timeling gone, Toby couldn't see a thing.

He thought about going back the way he came—but how would he find his way back in the dark? He was lost and alone in the Fortress of Evil.

"Hey!" he called in a high, panicky voice. "Hey, Blue Dude!"

The only answer was his own echo.

He thought he saw shapes in the darkness, slithering toward him, reaching for him. He backed up—and tripped.

"Aaaaggggghhhh!" he yelled as he fell onto his back. He struck the back of his head on something hard. His vision exploded in a shower of stars. He grabbed his head with both hands, groaning, "Dude! That hurt!"

Then he realized he was not lying on the stone floor of the Fortress. He was lying on a carpet of soft, yielding grass.

Toby opened his eyes—

"Yaaaggggghhhh!" he screamed, jumping to his feet.

He stood on a grassy hillside in bright sunlight. The air was as clear as crystal, as bright and sparkling as diamonds. Around him were grassy hills bordered by fragrant woods of acacia, cassia, jasmine, and sweet saso. In the distance, majestic snow-topped mountains rose against a clear, blue sky. From somewhere behind him, at the bottom of the slope, came the sounds of a gentle waterfall and a gurgling stream.

Toby had returned to the Garden of Eden, a place he had gone on his first trip in time with Max, Allie, and Grady.

He saw a glint of silver in the grass.

Whoa! he thought. *Déjà vu!*

Toby bent down, carefully parting the grass, and saw something long, shiny, and mirror-polished. It seemed to be made of pure sterling silver, but intricately detailed with perfectly formed scales, like the scales of a snake.

Toby followed the silvery snakelike thing up the hill and saw that it was encrusted with glittering white diamonds, red rubies, green emeralds, and blue sapphires. It led him to the mouth of a cave beside a grassy clearing. The mouth of the cave was half-hidden behind a curtain of trailing vines with red flowers.

This is crazy! Toby thought. *I've done all of this before! I know what's in that cave! I know what will happen if I reach out and push those vines aside!* But Toby couldn't help himself. He parted the vines with his hands—

And stared at a huge reptilian face of polished silver, with eyes of red fire. It was the face of the Dragon of Eden. A forked tongue flicked out between gleaming silvery fangs. Twin puffs of smoke blew from the Dragon's nostrils. The smoke forced Toby backward. He yelped and fell into a clump of flowering gorse.

Dude! Toby thought. *This is too weird! It's like I'm reliving everything that happened in the Garden of Eden!*

But in the next moment, the scene seemed to jump ahead in time. What he saw and experienced seemed both like and unlike his memory of the encounter with the Dragon of Eden. It was as if everything that was said and done was compressed into a series of highlights.

The Dragon lowered his head in a deep bow. "My name," he said, "is Lux. I have looked into your mind, Toby. I know what you want: power to rule over your friends, power to punish your enemies. And Toby, I can give you that power—if you will follow me. A dragon can be a powerful friend to have. I would always be there to serve you and do anything you ask."

"Anything?"

"Anything at all."

And as Toby and the Dragon continued talking, it soon stopped seeming weird. In fact, it seemed perfectly normal that Toby should be back in Eden, doing and saying things he had done and said before. It no longer surprised him that the Dragon, too, was playing his part, speaking his lines, as if performing a scene that was scripted long ago.

"As you grow older, and your dreams grow bigger," the Dragon continued, "I will be with you, helping to make all your dreams come true." In the next instant, Toby's mind was flooded with an image of himself as a great world leader. He was the Big Boss. If anyone opposed him—or even annoyed him—Toby could have that person punished on the spot.

"Your life can be so wonderful, Toby," the Dragon said, "with me as your friend."

"What do I have to do?" Toby asked.

"Just one little thing," the Dragon said. "Simply let me make an invisible mark on your forehead—a mark that only I can see."

In the next instant, the Silver Dragon reached out with his three-clawed forefoot. The longest claw touched Toby's forehead. A brilliant spark of light leaped from the claw to Toby's head. Toby shrieked and fell backward into the grass. And the darkness closed in around him.

"Do you remember that day, Toby?" said a voice from the darkness.

Toby opened his eyes. The light was gone. The Dragon was gone. The Garden was gone. He was back in the Fortress, surrounded by an utter blackness. Beneath his back was nothing but cold, hard stone. Toby groaned. "Who's there?"

"It is I, Ariyel," said the voice from the darkness.

Toby turned his head and saw the glowing Timeling standing a few feet away, gazing at him with golden eyes.

"Dude!" Toby said weakly. "Where have you been?"

"The question is," the Timeling said, "where have *you* been? Get up." The Timeling turned and began walking, not waiting for Toby.

"Hey!" Toby called. He jumped to his feet and hurried after Ariyel. "Hey, Blue Dude! Do you know what happened to me back there?"

"Of course," the Timeling said. "You fell and hit your head."

"I don't mean that," Toby said. "I mean the part where I went back to the Garden of Eden and saw—"

"Yes?" Ariyel said.

"Nothing," Toby said. "I guess I blacked out and had a dream. . . . Well, what happens now?"

"Now?" Ariyel said. "Would you like to see the 'now' that you have created?"

Toby scowled. "What do you mean?"

"Just this," Ariyel said. And the instant he said "this," the Fortress disappeared, the darkness disappeared—

Toby was in his own house.

He stood in his living room. In front of him, just a few steps away, were his mother and two uniformed policemen. Toby's mother was a short, plump woman with dark brown hair streaked with gray. Her face was lined with worry, and her eyes looked tired and scared. She nervously twisted and untwisted a dishtowel in her hands.

The two policemen were grim-faced. "We're real sorry," said one of them, a balding, fiftyish man with glasses. "We don't have any leads on your son."

"But Toby's been gone for seventeen days!" his mother said. "He can't have just disappeared from the face of the Earth!"

The other policeman was young and brown-skinned, with short black hair. "We've talked to your son's friends," he said. "They haven't seen him. Apparently, the last person to see your son was Mr. Merkel, the store owner."

Toby froze. What should he do? Run? Stand still? If the policemen turned and saw him, they'd arrest him for sure!

"It's my fault!" a voice said behind Toby.

Toby turned and saw—

My dad! he thought, panicking. His father sat on the living room sofa. The man was hunched over, his head in his hands, looking more miserable than Toby had ever seen him before.

"It's all my fault," Toby's father repeated. "I was never around. A boy needs to have his father around. I should have gotten a job where I could be home more." Toby's father raised his head and looked straight at Toby—

But no, he wasn't looking at Toby. He was looking *through* Toby. *He doesn't see me at all,* Toby thought in amazement. *It's like I'm not even here!*

"What are we going to do, Donna?" Toby's father asked. "What if he never comes home? How will I live with myself? I don't think I ever told him I love him."

Toby's jaw dropped. He felt a dull, aching pressure in his chest. He saw tears in his dad's eyes. Toby had never seen his dad cry before. Then Toby turned and saw tears rolling down his mother's face.

I never knew! Toby thought. *I never knew they cared about me!*

"Didn't you?" said a voice behind him.

Toby turned—

And stood face-to-face with Ariyel. They were surrounded by the blackness of the Fortress once more. "Your father doesn't talk about his feelings very much," Ariyel said. "But deep inside, I think you know he cares. You've stolen, run from the police, and gotten yourself completely lost. Even so, your parents love you and miss you. They want you back home."

"Why are you doing this?" Toby shouted. The sound of his voice echoed and re-echoed in the darkness. "Why are you making me see things I don't want to see?"

"Elyon wants you to know that you have a choice to make," Ariyel said.

"A choice?" Toby snapped. "What kind of choice?"

"Life," Ariyel said, "or death."

"Dude!" Toby said. "What are you talking about?"

"Life," Ariyel repeated, "or death." The Timeling started to fade into the darkness.

"Hey!" Toby said. "Hey! Don't leave me alone!"

But the Timeling was already gone. Once more, Toby Brubaker was alone in the dark—but the Timeling's last words continued to echo in his mind:

Life . . . or death.

9

ABSOLUTE POWER

Commander Wrye looked around at the faces of his crew. "Can anyone explain," he asked, "why there's a Volkswagen Beetle parked on the surface of Mars?"

"Maybe," Elsa Niemann said, straight-faced, "it ran out of gas."

Lia Medina giggled. Major Kuzmin laughed out loud.

The commander scowled. "That's not funny."

"Commander," Gerard Vachon said, trying not to laugh, "you can't be serious!"

"I asked all of you what you saw," Commander Wrye said, pointing to the image on Lia Medina's computer screen, "and you all agreed that it's a Volkswagen."

"We agreed that it *looks* like a Volkswagen," Elsa Niemann said with a strong German accent. "But let's be reasonable, Commander! Cars don't fly!" She grinned slyly, then added, "Not even *German* cars."

The commander clenched his jaw. "Lia," he said, "zoom in on that—that *thing*. See if you can sharpen the image."

The Brazilian woman tapped on her keyboard. The image on the screen got larger, but it didn't get any clearer. "I'm sorry, Commander. That's the best I can do."

"Doesn't that look like a rear bumper?" the commander asked, pointing at the image. "And look! You can clearly make out the windows, the fenders, the—"

"Commander," Hana Yamada said in her crisp Japanese accent. "The International Space Authority did not send us to Mars to bring back some wild tale about a Volkswagen on Mars."

"Hana's right," Major Kuzmin said. "If we return with a story like that, they'll lock us up in a padded room."

The commander thought for a moment, then he said, "Look, I know you all think I've lost my mind. I can't explain why there's a Volkswagen on Mars any more than you can—but there has to be a logical explanation. There has to be a logical reason why that UFO came so close to us, and why it shot past us at ninety-thousand miles an hour. There has to be a logical explanation for a mile-wide Face on Mars. Maybe when we solve those mysteries, we'll understand how Volkswagens can fly."

Allie turned and walked away from the campfire. As she passed the Timeling Jarael she avoided his searching, golden gaze.

Mr. O'Dell, warming his hands on the opposite side of the fire, looked up. "Allie," he asked, "where are you going?"

"Away," Allie said over her shoulder. "I need to think. Don't worry, I'll be back."

"Well, don't go far," Mr. O'Dell said. "I don't want to have to send out a search party."

"Ha-ha." Allie walked around a stand of shadowy trees and disappeared from view.

Mr. O'Dell turned to the Timeling, a look of helplessness on his face. "I don't know what to do for her," he said. "Everything I say is wrong."

"Stay here by the fire," Jarael said. "I'll look after her." He turned and followed Allie into the night-shadows of the forest.

Allie felt her way among the shadowy trees, keeping the lake on her right so she wouldn't get lost. She breathed deeply, filling her lungs with the scent of the trees, the scent of the earth—then she sighed sadly. Her sigh mingled with the sound of the breeze whispering through the pines.

Allie looked up at the sky, at the star-splashed road of the Milky Way—a road that stretched from horizon to horizon, seeming to lead all the way to heaven. *I wish I could talk to God right now*, she thought, *but I'm too mad, too hurt, too depressed—*

"Why don't you talk to Him? Right now, when you're

hurting, is when you need Him most." The voice had spoken so softly, so gently, that Allie didn't realize at first that someone had spoken to her. Then she turned around.

"Oh!" she said. "It's you!"

Jarael emerged from the night-shadows of the forest, wrapped in his pale blue glow. "He loves you," the Timeling said, "and He wants to help you—if you'll just let Him."

"Sorry," Allie said, "but I just don't feel like praying right now. In fact, I don't feel like talking, either, so if you'll excuse me—"

"Your father's worried about you, Allie," Jarael said, interrupting.

"Boy," Allie said, "you Timelings are not very good at taking a hint, are you? I'm trying to tell you that I *don't* want to talk—I just want to be left *alone*."

"Your father loves you, Allie," Jarael said.

"Oh, really? Well, he sure has a weird way of showing it." Allie turned and walked away from the Timeling, hoping he would get the message.

Jarael followed her. "Your father's not perfect," he said.

"You can say that again."

"He's self-centered," Jarael said. "And he's not very sensitive to other people's feelings."

"Bingo."

"But he does love you," Jarael said.

"Yeah, right." Allie turned her back on the Timeling and looked up at the sky. A big lump of hurt lodged in her throat, choking her.

"Allie," Jarael asked, "do you know what bitterness is?"

Allie didn't answer.

"Bitterness is a poison," Jarael said. "It poisons your relationship with God, and with people. It poisons your heart. It poisons your soul."

"Look," Allie said. "I know I have a lot of bitterness inside. But I can't help it. It hurts so much inside, and the hurt just won't go away."

"I know it hurts," Jarael said. "When someone has wounded you, as your father has wounded you, it hurts. It really hurts."

"I want the hurt to go away."

"I'm sorry," Jarael said, "but you *can't* make the hurt go away."

Allie turned and looked Jarael squarely in his soft, golden eyes. "Then what *can* I do?"

"You can choose not to be bitter."

"How?" Allie asked in a strangled voice. She brushed a tear from her cheek.

"You can choose to forgive your father."

"No!" Allie snapped, turning her back once more. "I won't forgive him! I won't! Not unless he changes! Not unless he comes home and puts our family back together again!"

"Allie," Jarael said softly, "he won't do that."

"He has to," Allie said, "or I won't forgive him."

"Then you will poison yourself with bitterness," Jarael said sadly. "When your father decided to seek a divorce, he hurt you. I know that. And Allie, there's nothing you can do about that. But when you decide not to forgive, you hurt yourself. You poison yourself."

"Leave me alone!" Allie said.

"I understand," Jarael said. "God understands. Give yourself time, Allie. Think about what I've told you. Pray about it. Tell God how you honestly feel—"

"Would you please just go!" Allie said. She whirled about, eyes flashing, ready to lash out at the Timeling—but Jarael was gone.

Allie had her wish. She was alone. Surrounded by the darkness of the night and the darkness of her pain, she began to cry softly.

Commander Wrye settled into the seat next to Major Kuzmin. "Vladimir," he said, "I've been thinking about the secret on Mars ever since we launched. Tell me—do you *really* believe civilization would collapse if we found evidence of an advanced alien race?"

"Some of our top scientists think so," Kuzmin said. "And I agree. I think people would say, 'We have nothing to strive for, nothing to believe in.' Society would fall apart. Science and industry would break down. Religion would collapse because people would lose faith in God."

"But why would people stop believing in God?" Wrye asked. "I used to read the Bible, and it plainly says that God created another intelligent race besides humans."

Kuzmin looked surprised. "The Bible says that God created an *alien* race?"

"Not aliens," the commander said. "*Angels.*"

"Angels! Humph!" Kuzmin snorted.

"I know you think God and angels don't exist," the commander said, gazing through the viewpane toward Mars. "But then, neither do flying Volkswagens."

The campfire was burning low. Mr. O'Dell crouched by the fire, poking the embers with a stick. He checked his watch. Allie had been gone for more than ten minutes. So had the Timeling. Mr. O'Dell was getting worried.

Allie thinks I don't love her, he thought, stroking his beard. *If only she knew how much I care. Just because I divorced her mother doesn't mean I don't love my own daughter.*

Another minute passed. Finally, Mr. O'Dell stood up and looked around. "Allie!" he called into the darkness.

No answer.

"Jarael!" he called. "Allie! Someone! Anyone!"

"I'm right here, Dad," said a voice behind him.

Mr. O'Dell turned and saw Allie walking out of the shadows, approaching the dying, flickering fire. He gave a sigh of relief.

"Where's Jarael?" Allie asked.

Mr. O'Dell eyed his daughter closely. She looked as if she had been crying. He felt a twinge of guilt. "I thought Jarael was with you," he said.

"He was," Allie said. "Then he left. I wonder where he—"

"Ah, you're back!" said a voice. Allie and her father turned and saw a blue glowing figure standing at the edge of the clearing. "Come on," Jarael said, beckoning to them. "Let's go."

Allie folded her arms. "Where are we going?"

"You'll see," Jarael said. "Come on."

Allie sighed. "All right. Let's go, Dad."

Mr. O'Dell nodded. He and Allie followed the Timeling away from the dying campfire. They climbed the wooded ridge with the lake on their left. Jarael led the way, lighting their path with his blue glow.

As they walked, Allie looked up at the moonless, starspattered sky. One star seemed especially bright—and red. That "star," Allie realized, was actually the planet Mars. For a moment, she felt a dizzy sensation. *Did Jarael actually transport Dad and me to Earth? Or are we still on Mars, experiencing some sort of illusion or hallucination?*

The trail led upward. As they climbed, the woods on either side became denser. The spicy fragrance of pine trees was intense along the trail. Allie breathed in the rich evergreen perfume as she walked.

After several minutes, Allie noticed that the pine fragrance had faded, and she could no longer hear the sighing of the wind in the pines. She looked up at the night sky—

And she gasped.

The stars were moving. That shouldn't happen. The stars in the sky don't move. Allie looked all around—and she knew she was no longer in the mountains near Clear

Lake. She was in outer space, strolling through the universe, hiking among the stars—and every step she took was light-years long.

Allie stopped, and her father bumped into her from behind. "Allie?" he said. "What is it?"

"Look around you," Allie said.

Up ahead, Jarael stopped and turned.

"Jarael," Allie said, "what's happening? Where are we?"

"We are on the starry pathway," the Timeling said.

"Where is it taking us?" Allie asked.

"To the place where everything will be revealed," Jarael said. "Come. It's not much farther." He turned and continued walking.

Her mind a jumble of questions, Allie moved forward. The stars seemed to move past her, as if she were walking through a forest of thousands and thousands of burning candles. She looked down and saw that the pathway beneath her feet was paved with shining stardust.

Ahead, a golden Light shone in the darkness of space. As Jarael walked in front of the two humans, the radiance of the golden Light passed through the Timeling's body as if he were made of blue stained glass.

They walked toward the Light for what seemed like a long time. Finally, the stardust path brought them to a place that was bordered by great billowing nebulas of hydrogen gas and stars of many colors and sizes. The stars ranged in appearance from blue-white diamonds to glowing red embers. The gas clouds were illuminated in a variety of shades—red, orange, yellow, green, blue, and violet.

Jarael stopped in the middle of the broad space between the hydrogen clouds. Allie and her father stopped, too.

"Hello, Allie," said a voice from the Light. The voice was gentle and soft, yet strong.

"Allie!" her father said in a shocked voice. "Who is that?"

"You know who I am, don't you, Allie?" the Light asked.

"Yes," Allie said. "I know."

"You've been avoiding Me," the Light said. "That's why I brought you here. We need to talk."

"I—" Allie hesitated, biting her lip. "I don't want to talk to You."

"You're angry with Me."

Allie nodded.

"Why?" the Light asked.

Allie shrugged—then tears welled in her eyes. "Don't You know?" she said accusingly. "My life is so messed up!"

"I know how hurt you feel," the Light said.

"I just don't understand what my life is supposed to be," Allie said. "I've had these really incredible experiences, you know? I time-traveled three times with Max, Grady, and Toby, and on each trip the most awesome things happened. Dangerous things, but wonderful things. We saw dinosaurs and a dragon, we saw a war in outer space, we got captured by knights and a crazy wizard, we got chased by robots—" Her voice choked.

"And then?" the Light prompted.

"And then," Allie said, "I came back home to the same old mess I left behind. My family fell apart. My dad never has time for me, and doesn't keep his promises. Now he's going to move away and marry a woman I can hardly stand!"

Allie paused and looked up at the Light. The golden radiance of the Light glinted in Allie's braces and in the tears that glistened in her eyes. "You know," she said, "when we went on those time-trips and got in all that trouble, I always felt so close to You! I mean, even when our lives were hanging by a thread, I always knew that we weren't alone—You were always with us."

"But when the adventure was over," the Light said, "you didn't feel close to Me anymore."

"Exactly!" Allie said. "I didn't feel You with me anymore. I'd be at home or at school, and I felt—" She paused, groping for words.

"Abandoned?" the Light said.

"That's it!" Allie said. "Abandoned. It was like You were there when I was jumping from one disaster to another—and that was really cool. But then I came home and had to deal with my mom being an emotional wreck and my dad ignoring me and his girlfriend being snotty to me and I was sad and depressed and having trouble with my schoolwork. Where were You then?"

"I was with You," the Light said. "I was always with You."

"Then why didn't I *feel* you with me?" Allie said. "Why did I feel so alone?"

"Allie, I am always there," the Light said, "whether you feel My presence or not. My love for you *never* changes."

"Then why can't I believe that?" Allie said.

"That's not hard to understand," the Light said. "You see

your father breaking his promises. You feel abandoned by him. You feel you can't trust him."

Allie's father frowned. "Now, just a doggone—"

"And deep down," the Light continued, "you think that if you can't trust your earthly father, then maybe you can't trust your heavenly Father, either. Believe Me, Allie, I will never break My promises to you. I will never abandon you. I am always with you."

"If that's true," Allie said, "then why don't You answer my prayers?"

"Allie," the Light said, "I have answered every prayer you ever prayed. When you asked for something good, My answer was 'Yes.' When you asked for something that was not good, My answer was, 'Wait—I'll give you something even better.'"

"That's not true!" Allie said. "I asked You again and again for something good—but You won't give it to me! I've asked You to put my family back together again! How can You tell me that's not good? How can You say 'No' to that prayer?"

"Allie," the Light said, "does your father want your family to be together again?"

Allie turned to her father. "Well, Dad?"

Mr. O'Dell scowled. "Look, I can't help it if her mother and I can't get along!"

The Light grew brighter, and focused on Mr. O'Dell like a spotlight.

"Okay, okay!" Mr. O'Dell said, shielding his eyes with his hand and looking away. "The truth is—I just want to marry Penelope and get on with my life."

"Allie," the Light said, "that is your father's choice."

"But—," Allie spluttered. "But it's *wrong* to break up a family!"

"What would you have Me do?" the Light said.

"Make my dad do the right thing," Allie said. "Make him put our family back together."

"You want Me to overrule your father's free will?" the Light asked.

"Yes!" Allie said. "That's exactly what I want!"

"You know I will not do that," the Light said.

"Then give me the power to do it!" Allie demanded, her eyes flashing in defiance.

"Allie!" her father said in a shocked voice.

"You don't understand what you are asking," the Light said.

"Yes, I do!" Allie said. "I want the power to make my dad do the right thing."

"Very well, then," the Light said. "The power is yours."

Allie blinked in surprise. "Really?"

"Hey!" her father said. "Whoa! Hold on! You can't do that!"

"Allie O'Dell," the Light said—and the voice seemed strangely sad. "You now hold an awesome power in your hands—a power that I Myself have chosen never to use. It is the power to overrule human free will."

"I can hardly believe it," Jarael said in a stunned voice. "No human being has ever been given such power!"

"Hold on!" Mr. O'Dell said. "I have the right to make my own decisions!"

"Dad," Allie said.

Mr. O'Dell turned to Allie. "What?"

"Be quiet," Allie said.

Mr. O'Dell shut his mouth.

"Now, come give me a hug," Allie said.

"Okay, Allie," Mr. O'Dell said. He walked over to Allie and gave her a hug. As his arms wrapped around her, she looked up into her father's face. *I can't believe it!* she thought. *It's true! He'll do anything I say!*

Allie stepped back and looked at her father. "You know, Dad, divorcing Mom was a really bad idea."

Her father nodded. "You're right, Allie," he said. "It was a terrible idea. I don't know what I was thinking. Your mother and I belong together."

Allie's eyes widened. "This is so awesome!" she said, turning to face the Light. "I don't know how to thank You for—"

But the Light was gone.

Allie turned to Jarael, a baffled look on her face. "Where did—?"

"I think you will find," Jarael said somberly, "that having the power to control another person's will is not as 'awesome' as you think it is."

Allie stubbornly set her jaw. "I don't care!" she said. "I'm going to have a family again! I'm going to have a dad who keeps his promises! That's all that matters to me!"

She was about to find out how wrong she was.

10

THE SUPREME LEADER

Commander Wrye clipped the tether from the belt of his jumpsuit to the lock-ring next to the computer terminal. He tapped on the keyboard. In a fraction of a second, the computer displayed three lines:

```
*** TOP SECRET ***
PROJECT THUVIA ARCHIVES
CYDONIA FILES
```

Using the computer's trackball, Commander Wrye pointed to a link and clicked. An image appeared on the screen—an image of the Face on Mars. The Face was humanlike, but not human. It was incredibly huge—1.6 miles long, 1.2 miles wide, and a third of a mile high. The expression seemed intelligent, but reptilian, even snake-like. Commander Wrye thought of it as an extee face—

"extee" was the term people at NASA used for "extraterrestrial" or alien.

He clicked the image to zoom in. The Face was cracked and crumbled in places. The pits of its eyes and nostrils and the vast trench of its mouth were partly filled in by windblown sands.

"There are a thousand questions written on that Face," a voice behind him said.

Commander Wrye turned and saw Mission Specialist Elsa Niemann floating toward him. She was a language and culture expert, representing the European Union, and she spoke with a German accent. When Spaceship *Thuvia* reached Mars, it would be her job to translate any alien writings they might find. Her blond hair was bound in a hair net. Her blue eyes keenly studied the image of the Face.

"Who carved it and when?" she continued. "What were they like? Is it the face of a Martian king? A Martian god? A demon? And what happened to the beings who carved it? Where are they now?"

"If the answers can be found," Commander Wrye said, "we'll find them."

"Even if the answers destroy us?" Elsa Niemann asked.

"Yes," Commander Wrye answered.

Toby was alone in the dark.

Ariyel, his Timeling guide, had left him. The last words

Ariyel had spoken rang in Toby's thoughts: *Elyon wants you to know that you have a choice to make: life . . . or death.*

Toby felt a surge of panic. He had always hated the dark—and this was total darkness, a darkness so complete he couldn't see his own hand in front of his eyes. He swore, cursing the Timeling who had brought him into some unknown corner of the Fortress and left him alone.

Toby had never felt more lost in his entire life. He wasn't just lost in the dark. He was lost in a strange place called Cydonia, lost on an alien planet, thirty-eight million miles from home.

Refusing to let himself cry, he jammed his hands into the pockets of his bulky jacket—and felt the clatter of plastic objects rattling inside. He reached into the lining and rummaged around. He felt CD cases, video-game cartridges, packages of batteries, a Nintendo Game Boy—

Dude! Toby pulled out the Game Boy and a package of AA batteries, then sat down on the stone floor. He broke open the package, spilling batteries all around him. Finally, he got two batteries loaded into the Game Boy and turned it on. The screen lit up. It wasn't much light, but it was better than nothing—especially now that his eyes had become adjusted to the dark. He stood up and shone the faint light around him, trying to figure out which way he had come.

By the pale light of the handheld video game, Toby saw that he was in a large, stone-walled hall. The walls were carved with reptilian shapes and scenes of space battles and exploding worlds. Several corridors led away from the room, winding away into other rooms filled with utter darkness.

Toby pointed the Game Boy at the floor and saw that the floor was caked with dust—and his sneakers had left tracks in the dust. *Excellent!* he thought. *I can retrace my steps!*

Holding the Game Boy at knee level, he followed the tracks. He came upon patches of bare stone floor and almost lost the tracks. After a few more minutes, the dust simply stopped. And so did the tracks.

Toby shone the Game Boy around, but there were no more tracks anywhere. He stopped, panic rising. Now he felt more lost than ever. He raised the Game Boy and shone its light all around him—

And he saw the door.

A door?

Toby walked up to the door and took a closer look. By the light of the Game Boy, he saw that it was a perfectly ordinary-looking door. It was painted white, and its hinges and knob were made of shiny, polished brass. The door was set into a white-painted doorframe in a plastered white wall.

Holding the Game Boy higher, Toby caught a glint of brass in the upper part of the door—a shiny brass plaque. There were words etched into the metal plaque—and Toby was astonished to see that the words were in English. The plaque read:

OFFICE OF THE
SUPREME LEADER

"The Supreme Leader?" Toby said aloud. "The Supreme Leader of what?"

He grasped the brass knob, expecting it to be locked. To his surprise, the knob turned easily and the door swung silently on well-oiled hinges. The room beyond the door was flooded with light.

Squinting, Toby turned off the Game Boy, walked into the room, and closed the door behind him. In a few moments, his eyes adjusted to the light.

The "Office of the Supreme Leader" (whoever that might be) was large and richly furnished. The walls and the high ceiling were white. Directly in front of Toby, a massive desk dominated one end of the room. Sunlight streamed through windows behind the desk.

The wall to Toby's right had twelve large, built-in video screens. The screens displayed an assortment of maps, charts, and reports. Toby was unable to make any sense of the information on the screens.

The wall to Toby's left featured a huge painting of a man in a dark business suit, standing in front of some draperies, with one hand resting on a globe of the world. The painting was so huge that the frame went from floor to ceiling, and the man in the painting was even larger than life-size. Toby couldn't help staring. There was something familiar about the man in the painting.

The man had short, bristly hair, skin that was pale and doughy, a pug nose, and cruel green eyes set in a bulky, brutish face. An arrogant sneer twisted the man's lips.

As Toby stared at that face—a face so strange yet so

familiar—he felt dizzy. There was a ringing in his ears, and he saw stars swarming like fireflies at the edge of his vision. *What's happening to me?* he wondered.

Toby staggered to the desk and steadied himself with both hands. The room seemed to revolve.

He looked down at his hands and gasped. They were not his hands! He turned the hands over, flexing the fingers. They were the hands of a grown man.

Stunned, Toby walked behind the desk and stood before the window. He gazed at his own reflection in the glass—but the face he saw was not his own face. It was the face of the man in the painting. Toby didn't know how it had happened, but he had somehow become transformed from a middle-schooler into a grown man. It had happened when he opened the white door and stepped into the room.

Suddenly, strange thoughts cascaded through his brain. Toby remembered being in the Fortress on Mars—but that was decades ago. Now, he was a man—the most powerful man in the world. Suddenly, he understood the meaning of the maps, charts, and reports on the video screens. They were reports from around the world—reports on the wars he had ordered, on the nations he had invaded, on the cities his bombers and missiles had turned to rubble. He wondered how he could have forgotten—even for a moment—who he was and how powerful he was!

He remembered how it all began. A long time ago, he had traveled in Max McCrane's Timebender back to the Garden of Eden. There he had met the Dragon of Eden. "As you grow older," the Dragon had told him, "I will be with you, helping to make all your dreams come true. Simply let me make an invisible mark on your forehead— a mark that only I can see. Let me place my seal upon you—and my power will always be there to serve you."

As Toby recalled those words, his eyes focused beyond his reflection in the window. Looking out the window, he saw that his dream had indeed come true. From the Supreme Leader's office, high atop a massive tower over- looking a city square, Toby could see a huge bronze statue, a statue of the Supreme Leader himself, Toby Brubaker.

A grin spread across his face. He rubbed an itchy spot on his forehead—the same place where the Dragon had placed his invisible mark. "I remember now," he said aloud—and he was surprised by the sound of his own voice. It was a deep voice, the voice of a man. "Yes, I remember—!"

He had come to power during a time of national crisis, when millions of people had no jobs and no money for food, when the nation faced a threat of war and terror and rebellion. The people wanted a strong leader to seize con- trol of the government and lead the nation out of its crisis.

And Tobias Rex was that man.

Yes, he remembered that he had changed his name from Toby Brubaker to Tobias Rex—a name of strength, a name of power, a name that meant "king." While the nation was reeling in crisis, he dissolved the old Constitution, dis- missed the Congress, and made himself Supreme Leader for life.

For years, the Dragon had remained invisibly at his side,

giving him advice, advancing his cause, arranging events and circumstances, helping Tobias Rex gain more and more power. Soon, the armies of Tobias Rex were marching into Canada and Mexico, and down through Central America and South America. He signed peace treaties with other nations—then he broke those treaties and sent his army, navy, and air force out to conquer them. Years passed. The forces of Tobias Rex took control of the Pacific Rim and parts of Europe and Africa.

Now he was preparing for his greatest conquest ever: a three-pronged attack against the Asian Federation. Tobias Rex and his advisers had devised a plan to launch an attack from the sea against the eastern flank and a land assault against the western flank, while a swarm of nuclear and antimatter weapons would be launched from submarines in the Indian Ocean to kill millions and strike terror into the heart of the enemy.

The desk communicator beeped and the screen lit up. "Hail the Supreme Leader," the man in the communicator screen said. "The prisoner has been brought under guard, as you ordered."

"Good," Tobias Rex said. "Send him in."

A few seconds later, the door of the office opened and four guards entered, leading a prisoner. The guards were heavily armed and clad in tan fatigues and chrome-silver helmets. The prisoner wore a black outfit, loose-fitting like pajamas. His hands were handcuffed in front of him, and his legs were bound by steel ankle bracelets.

"So, Jack Cade," Tobias Rex said. "We finally meet face-to-face." He stood up and came around his desk, approaching the prisoner. "The Rebellion is finished—and so are you. I have conquered half the world. Soon I will conquer the other half—and you'll be dead."

"Go ahead," the rebel leader said. "Torture me, execute me—if you can."

"I can," Tobias Rex said, "and I will." In a flash, he remembered the hundreds of enemies who had been arrested, imprisoned, tortured, and executed. Hundreds more had vanished without a trace. Anyone who had ever gotten in the way of Tobias Rex had been ruthlessly eliminated.

"You have no idea what is about to happen," Jack Cade said. "Soon I will be Supreme Leader—and you will be destroyed."

Tobias Rex threw back his head and laughed.

Jack Cade smiled as if he knew a secret Tobias Rex didn't know.

"Get this garbage out of my sight," Tobias Rex said, scowling.

The guards grabbed Cade, but he just grinned and rubbed a spot in the middle of his forehead, as if he felt an itch there.

The Supreme Leader's eyes widened. As he stared, the guards led the rebel leader through the door and out of sight. The Supreme Leader slammed the door shut. Then he turned and shouted, "Dragon! I summon you!"

A flash of light!

The air crackled. The light solidified into a silvery four-legged beast. It was twice as massive as an elephant, and had a long, snaking neck and thousands of mirrorlike scales. Its wings spread out and filled the office from wall to wall. Its legs, body, and tail were encrusted with gleaming gemstones. Its eyes blazed with red fire. Smoke curled from its nostrils and a serpentlike tongue lolled between silvery fangs.

"Yes, Toby?" the Silver Dragon said.

"I told you not to call me that!" the Supreme Leader said. "I'm Tobias Rex!"

"Let's not quibble," the Dragon said. "Get to the point. Time is short."

"*Whose* time is short?" Tobias Rex asked.

The Dragon smiled evilly. "Yours," he said.

"What are you talking about?" Tobias Rex said. "We have a deal! I received your mark, and you have to serve me!"

"I have kept my end of the bargain," the Dragon said.

"No, you haven't!" Tobias Rex said, slamming his fist against the desk. "You sold me out!"

"Did I?" the Dragon said, scratching his chin with one silver foreclaw.

"The leader of the Rebellion was just here," Tobias Rex said.

"Ah," the Dragon said. "Jack Cade."

"You made a deal with him!" Tobias Rex said. "The same deal you made with me. Don't try to deny it."

"Why should I deny it?" the Dragon said, exhaling a puff of smoke. "Of course I made a deal with Jack Cade."

"You can't do that!" Tobias Rex shouted. "I command you to—"

The Dragon belched flame. Toby screamed and ducked.

"You never understood our bargain, did you?" the Dragon growled. "When you received my mark, you stupidly thought that you controlled me when it was always the other way around. Well, Jack Cade has received my mark now—and I don't need you anymore."

"You're wrong!" Tobias Rex said. "You still need me. Cade's a dead man. I just sent him out to be executed!"

"You gave the order," the Dragon said, "but it was not carried out. Unfortunately for you, the men who guarded Cade were not very trustworthy. Jack Cade is already a free man—and he will soon be the Supreme Leader instead of you."

"But you promised to serve me for life!" Tobias Rex said.

The Dragon laughed, and flames exploded from his mouth. "Yes," the Dragon said, "and I have kept my word. But here's the catch: Your life is now over."

Whump! The building shook. Chunks of plaster fell from the ceiling.

The Supreme Leader ran around the desk and looked out the window. A column of heavy black tanks crawled up the street, bristling with cannon muzzles and rocket tubes. On a single cue, the tanks fired. Rockets smashed into the massive statue of the Supreme Leader. The statue exploded into millions of white-hot fragments.

Tobias Rex screamed and fell back from the window. Glass shattered. Flaming statue fragments zipped across the room and clanged against the opposite wall.

"Dragon!" the Supreme Leader called out. "Do something! Make them stop!"

"Why would I want them to stop?" the Dragon said. "This is the place your choices have brought you, Toby. You chose to accept my mark. Now you must accept the consequences of your choices—just as I soon will."

"What are you talking about?" the Supreme Leader asked.

"A time is coming soon," the Dragon said, "when I must go into the Pit. That is the sentence I received for my rebellion against Elyon the Most High. But I have sworn to take as many human beings with me as I can—and that includes *you*."

"No!" Tobias Rex sobbed, shaking his head. "No! I don't want to die! I don't want to go there!" He turned his back on the Dragon and looked up to the ceiling. "God! Please, listen to me! I'm sorry! Help me!"

Thwack!

The Dragon's tail knocked Tobias Rex facedown on the carpet. "It's too late to switch sides," the beast said, snarling. "Do you think you can change the past? Do you think you can undo all the choices you have made? Do you think you can wish it away as if it never happened? You have received my mark! You belong to me!"

Tobias Rex struggled to his feet. "This can't be happening! I have to wake up!"

"This is not a dream!" the Dragon roared. "This is the life you have chosen! This is the reality you have made! Deal with it!"

Another explosion rocked the building. Ceiling plaster rained down. The floor shook beneath the Supreme

Leader's feet. He stood in the middle of his office, paralyzed with fear and indecision. *What do I do now?* he asked himself.

Over the Dragon's roar and the thundering rockets, a thought came to his mind, a message from long ago: *Elyon wants you to know that you have a choice to make—life or death.* And Toby Brubaker knew, as his entire world crumbled around him, that he had made the wrong choice.

11

SURFING THE SPACE WAVES

Max and Grady knelt on the rocky ledge beside the deep Martian canyon, praying for Toby Brubaker. Toby wasn't exactly the kind of person they would call a "friend." They didn't even like him. After all, who could like a person who stole, lied, cheated, and was nasty and obnoxious to everyone around him? But Max and Grady knew that God loved Toby—so they prayed for him.

"Rise, my young friends," Zaykiel the Timeling said. "The Most High is pleased with your prayers."

"What about Allie?" Grady said. "And what about Toby? Are they going to be okay? Did they make the right choices?"

"That has not been revealed to me," Zaykiel said. "I have told you all I know. Come. Let's return to your vehicle. I have much more to show you."

The Timeling led them back through the narrow gap

between the two rock walls. As they walked, Grady asked, "Zaykiel, could you explain something?"

"Perhaps," Zaykiel said. "What is your question?"

"It's about prayer," Grady said. "I don't understand why we need to pray. I mean, God knows everything, right? He knows what we're going to pray for before we even ask Him. He even knows what's the best thing for us, so when we ask Him for the wrong thing, He says 'No' to our prayers."

"That's right," the Timeling said.

"So why does God even want us to pray?" Grady asked. "Why does God want us to ask Him for help, when He already knows better than we do what kind of help we need?"

"Ah," Zaykiel said. "To understand prayer, you must first understand why the universe was created. When you understand the meaning of Creation, you will understand the meaning of prayer."

Grady and Max stopped and exchanged glances. They read the same question in each other's eyes: *What does the creation of the universe have to do with prayer?*

"Come along," Zaykiel called over his shoulder. "All will be clear to you soon."

They emerged from the cleft between the rock walls and walked out into the valley where Timebender sat. To Max, the car seemed to be waiting for them, eager to take them somewhere. They got in the car, Max and Grady in front, Zaykiel in back.

"Let's go," the Timeling said.

"Go where?" Max asked.

The Timeling pointed straight up. "Out there."

Max lifted Timebender off the surface of Mars and headed for the sky. Within minutes, they were so high that the sky had turned a dark blue-violet and the horizon appeared curved instead of flat. "How far up are we going?" Max asked.

"All the way up," the Timeling replied.

Max and Grady looked at each other—then shrugged.

Timebender continued climbing. The blue-violet sky turned black, strewn with stars. Grady pointed out the passenger-side window. There, one shining "star" moved swiftly against a background of unmoving stars. "What's that?" he asked.

"That is Phobos," Zaykiel said, "one of the two moons of Mars. Your scientists have named the other moon Deimos. It's on the far side of the planet right now."

They continued on, higher up, farther out, deeper into the sky. Behind them, Mars became a blotchy, rust-red disk. Ahead of them, stretching across the sky, the Milky Way shone like a starry roadway, inviting the soaring Volkswagen to roam the universe.

"Where are we going?" Max asked.

"To the edge of Creation," Zaykiel said.

"Commander!" shouted Lia Medina. "Commander Wrye!"

Commander Wrye floated up from the galley, where he

had fixed himself a bulb of coffee. "Coming," he said. "What is it?"

"The Volks—I mean, the UFO!" she said. "It's moving again. Here's the long-range scan." She pointed to her computer screen.

"Speed and heading?" the Commander asked.

"Forty kilometers per second," Lia Medina said. "Straight into space. It passed within twenty miles of Phobos and then—*poof!*—it disappeared from the scanner."

The commander shook his head in amazement. "Well," he said, "if you see that Volkswagen again, make sure you get its license number. Whoever's behind the wheel of that thing should get a ticket for speeding."

Timebender streaked across the solar system in absolute silence.

"What's that?" Grady asked, pointing beyond the windshield.

Max looked where Grady pointed. Ahead were a number of tiny points of light that moved across the background of unmoving stars.

"That's the asteroid belt," Max said. "Remember when we were here before? We saw the Enemy's forces land on a planet between Mars and Jupiter."

"Yeah," Grady said. "And the planet exploded. The asteroid belt is all that was left—just a bunch of big rocks in orbit between Mars and Jupiter."

Timebender sped on toward the asteroid belt. Soon the points of light were close enough to be seen as distinct shapes. When Max saw they were heading straight into the asteroid belt, he turned to Zaykiel and said, "Shouldn't we go *around* the asteroids?"

"There is nothing to fear," Zaykiel said as Timebender plunged on.

Flash! An explosion of light blossomed in front of the car.

Max and Grady shouted and covered their eyes—but Timebender was undamaged. "What was that?" Grady asked.

"A tiny asteroid fragment," Zaykiel said. "It vaporized itself against the protective shield I placed around your vehicle."

With shaky hands, Max pulled the asthma inhaler from his pocket and took a puff.

Flash! . . . FLASH! . . . FLASH!

More asteroid fragments exploded in cascades of light as Timebender zoomed through the asteroid field and beyond. Ahead, a planet came into view—a gas giant banded by swirled ribbons of color. In the southern hemisphere was a great red oval, with clouds swirling around it.

"That's Jupiter!" Max said.

"Yes," the Timeling said. "When the Enemy destroyed the planet that became the asteroid belt, one large piece of the planet crashed into Jupiter. That collision formed a vast storm system in Jupiter's atmosphere—"

"That big red spot!" Max said.

"Yes," Zaykiel said. "That 'spot' is actually a vast hurricane, three times as wide as the diameter of your Earth. It has swirled like that for thousands of years, and it will continue to swirl until the End of All Things."

Timebender cruised past the massive face of Jupiter—a planet eleven times the diameter of Earth. The rings of Jupiter, much thinner than the great rings of Saturn, looked like a rainbow that encircled the planet.

"I've always wondered why God made the universe so big," Max said. "I mean, why did Elyon make planets way out here where nobody lives?"

"Every object in the universe has a purpose," Zaykiel said. "Every electron, every planet, every galaxy is part of Elyon's Eternal Plan. Don't you know why Elyon created the planet you call Jupiter?"

Max and Grady shook their heads.

"Jupiter is the guardian of your solar system," Zaykiel said. "Its mass equals that of three hundred Earths, creating a huge gravity field that sweeps the solar system clean of comets, asteroids, and meteors."

"Cool!" Grady said. "Jupiter is like a cosmic vacuum cleaner, sucking up space debris so it won't destroy Earth."

"Exactly," Zaykiel said.

Without warning, Timebender took a sharp turn away from Jupiter, accelerating swiftly. Looking in the rearview mirror, Max saw Jupiter shrink to the size of a coin, then to a dot, then to nothing at all.

"Zaykiel," Max said. "We're—we're leaving the solar system!"

It was true. The stars in front of them blurred and blended into a swirl of colors. Timebender sailed through this neon whirlpool for several minutes, then—

Timebender stopped. It didn't slow down. It simply stopped.

Max and Grady looked out the passenger-side window and saw a sight of incredible beauty and brilliance. It looked like a vast pinwheel of light. "That," Zaykiel said, "is your home, the Milky Way—a spiral-shaped galaxy of more than a hundred billion stars. And look out there."

Max and Grady looked all around and saw a universe filled with pinwheel galaxies, ball-shaped galaxies, and irregular-shaped galaxies. "So many galaxies," Max said in an awed voice. "And among them all, billions of light-years of empty space."

"We're so far from home," Grady said. "It makes me feel—kind of homesick."

"I brought you here for a reason," Zaykiel said. "I want you to understand your place in the universe."

"Our place in the universe?" Max said. "What do you mean?"

"As you go through life," the Timeling said, "people will tell you that the universe is big and you are small. They will say that, in the grand scheme of the universe, you are nothing but a flyspeck. They will tell you that there is no God, and no Eternal Plan."

"I don't care what anyone tries to tell me," Grady said. "I know that God is real. I know He cares about us."

"Good," the Timeling said. "Because He loves you more than you know. You hold an eternal place in His heart."

Max and Grady looked around them at the wide, wide universe. The light from a trillion stars fell upon their faces and sparkled in their eyes.

"Wow," Grady said.

"Awesome," Max said. And it was probably the first time Max had ever said that word in such a meaningful way.

"Yes," the Timeling said. "It is awesome. But there's more."

"More?" Max said. "What else could there be?"

"I have taken you deep into space," Zaykiel said. "Now I shall take you deep into time—deeper than you have ever been before. Are you ready?"

A grin spread across Grady's face. "Let's go," he said.

With that, the universe began to shrink. The galaxies moved closer and closer together. Eons of time rolled backward. Galaxies turned into formless clouds of hydrogen.

Max looked at Zaykiel. The Timeling's eyes shone with a golden radiance. Then Max understood: The Timeling was enjoying this ride as much as they were! Zaykiel was doing what he loved to do, what he was created to do—soaring through time and space in the service of Elyon. To the Timeling, this trip was like a roller-coaster ride, only better—it was more exciting, more thrilling, more *fun* than any ride at any amusement park. Like the golden warmth of the sun, joy radiated from Zaykiel's innermost being, warming Max's own soul.

"Look, Max!" Grady shouted, tugging at Max's sleeve. "The universe is shrinking! It's the Big Bang in reverse!"

"Yes," Zaykiel said. "The universe is flowing back in time to the moment of Creation. Watch!"

Great masses of stars drew closer together, compacted into a single mass, then shrank into a ball of light, space, and time. The ball shrank to a point—then disappeared completely. Everything was darkness, silence, and timelessness.

"What happens now?" Max whispered.

"We wait," Zaykiel said.

"For what?" Grady whispered.

"The Beginning," Zaykiel said.

Max and Grady waited. Eternity waited. Then . . .

The Word shouted into the timeless darkness.

Let there be LIGHT!

And there was LIGHT!

The Word shattered the darkness. Light blossomed forth. Time came into being, expanding at the speed of love.

The universe swelled in size, white-hot and violent, yet smooth and delicately balanced. The Word carefully controlled the force of the explosion, fine-tuning it to an accuracy of one part in a trillion trillion. The complex code for the creation of life and intelligence was written into the structure of the elements.

As the universe expanded, Zaykiel sent the Volkswagen Beetle soaring, sailing, surfing across cresting waves of star gas, diving through billowing swells of cosmic radiation. Max and Grady saw solar systems forming and planets whirling. All around them, Creation blossomed in an array of brilliant colors and dazzling energies, in nebulas and gas clouds, in hydrogen and helium, in carbon and oxygen. Then—

Life! Creation abounded in life!

Timebender soared over worlds that looked like Earth but were not Earth. Grady and Max saw green-and-blue planets with oxygen atmospheres and wispy white clouds of water. Living creatures, strange and beautiful, swam through oceans of clear water, or crawled in oozing swamps, or migrated across grassy plains. Everywhere they looked, Max and Grady saw evidence of the Creator's artistry.

"There, Grady!" Zaykiel said. "There is your answer."

Grady looked perplexed. "The answer to what?"

"Your question about prayer," Zaykiel said. "Remember? I told you that, to understand prayer, you must first understand why the universe was created. When you understand the meaning of Creation, you will understand the meaning of prayer."

"I don't under—," Grady began—then his eyes lit up. "Wait! I think I get it!"

"Of course, my young friends!" Zaykiel said. "The answer is all around you, right before your eyes!"

"I think I get it, too!" Max said. "Elyon created the universe to bring forth life—"

"Yeah," Grady said. "And not just plants and animals, but people! Living souls!"

"Yes, yes!" Zaykiel said. "Souls who have a will of their

own and are free to love Him or reject Him. He wants the fellowship and friendship of beings who are like Him but different from Him, separate from Him but connected to Him. He wants fellowship, communion, and—"

"Prayer!" Grady said. "Elyon created the universe so that there would be prayer!"

"Exactly!" the Timeling said. "Now you know why the universe exists—to bring forth prayer!"

"Whoa!" Max said. "I don't know why I didn't see it before!" He looked out at the shining universe with a new sense of wonder.

"I always thought," Grady said, "that prayer is about asking God for the things I want—'God, gimme this' and 'God, gimme that.' But it's more than that, isn't it?"

"Yes, Grady," the Timeling said, "much more. Prayer is sharing your happiness and your sorrow with Him, telling Him about your hopes and dreams. And it is not just talking to Him—it's listening to Him as well. Prayer is an endless conversation with God." Zaykiel paused.

"What is it?" Max said.

The Timeling seemed to be listening to a voice only he could hear.

"Is something wrong?" Grady asked.

"It's time to go back," Zaykiel said at last. "And I want you both to pray for Allie."

"Allie!" Grady said. "What's wrong with Allie?"

"Yeah," Max said. "What should we pray for?"

"Just pray," Zaykiel said. "Join your will to the will of Elyon. He knows what Allie needs right now."

So Max and Grady prayed for Allie as Timebender sped through the cosmos. They traveled a path of stardust between mountains of rainbow-colored clouds. Then Max and Grady heard it: a high wail of despair.

"That's Allie!" Grady said.

Timebender came around a stardust curve and stopped in the middle of a broad space bordered by starry nebulas. There, in the space between the stars, stood Allie O'Dell, Roger O'Dell, and the Timeling named Jarael. Something was very, very wrong. Allie's face was in her hands, and she cried uncontrollably. Max and Grady jumped out of the car.

"Allie!" Grady called as he ran past Mr. O'Dell. "Allie, what's wrong?"

Allie looked up. Tears streamed down her face. "Grady! Max!" she called.

Grady reached Allie first, and she clung to him.

"What have I done?" she sobbed. "It's horrible! Horrible!"

Max ran past Mr. O'Dell, then he stopped and took a closer look at the man. "Oh, no!" he said, backing away. "Allie, what happened to your dad?"

Grady turned and looked at Allie's father, and his eyes opened wide with shock.

Mr. O'Dell looked much as he had looked before, except that his face seemed as if it had been carved from wood. His hair and beard seemed painted on with bright, glossy, orange-red paint. His chin was on a hinge—it flapped up and down when he talked.

"Hello, Max. Hello, Grady." Mr. O'Dell said in a lifeless

voice. His eyeballs slid back and forth, like the eyes of a ventriloquist's dummy.

"Jarael," Max said. "What happened to Mr. O'Dell?"

The Timeling's voice was filled with sadness. "Allie has received the power she asked for," he said.

"But I didn't know!" Allie cried. "I just wanted my dad to do the right thing!"

"Yes," Roger O'Dell said woodenly. "The right thing, the right thing. Whatever you say, Allie dear."

"I didn't think anything like this would happen!" Allie said. "I didn't know I would turn my own father into a—a—" She couldn't finish the sentence.

"A puppet," Grady said in an anguished voice.

"A puppet," Roger O'Dell said, raising his hand as if someone had pulled his strings. "I am your puppet, Allie dear, yours to command."

Allie bit her knuckles. "Oh," she sobbed, "I've made such a mess of things!"

Max turned to Jarael. "What can she do to change him back?"

Jarael walked over to Allie. "Do you want him as he was?"

"Of course I do!" Allie said. "I don't want a puppet for a father!"

"But if he becomes what he once was," Jarael said, "he will no longer be yours to control. Are you sure you want him as he was?"

"I . . ." Allie hesitated, taking one more look at her father's wooden face and vacant eyes, the mouth that moved up and down like the mouth of a dummy. "Yes," she said, shuddering. "I'm sure."

"Good," Jarael said. "You know, God created human beings with the ability to think and choose. He gives you that freedom so you will be a real person, not a puppet. Without that freedom, you can't be truly human."

"I know," Allie said. "I guess if my dad is ever going to change, if he's ever going to be the kind of father I want him to be, he'll have to make that decision himself. I can't make it for him."

"That's true," Jarael said.

"And," Allie said, "I guess that means he may *never* change."

"That's also true," Jarael said. "But you mustn't give up praying for him."

"I won't give up," Allie said.

"I know you won't," Jarael said.

"Ugghhh!" Roger O'Dell groaned. Then, as if he were a marionette with its strings cut, he collapsed onto the glittering expanse of stars.

Allie, Grady, and Max rushed to his side. Allie cradled his head in her arms. Mr. O'Dell's eyes fluttered open. "Oh, Allie," he said. "What happened? I must have passed out or—" He paused, as if he remembered something— something horrible. He looked around with wide, staring eyes. "Where are we?" he asked.

"I don't know," Allie said, looking up, expecting to see stars and clouds of hydrogen. Instead, she saw—

The interior of the Fortress. They were back in the arena

of the Fortress. Allie, Grady, and Max were huddled around Mr. O'Dell. Zaykiel and Jarael stood a few steps away. And behind them sat Timebender.

Max got to his feet and turned to Zaykiel. "What happens now?" he said. "Can we go home?"

"Wait, Max!" Allie said. "What about Toby? We can't go home without Toby!"

12

NOTHING IS IMPOSSIBLE

He couldn't remember his name. He remembered the noise—explosive, ear-splitting noise. He remembered the smell of smoke and the sound of flying bomb fragments and raining debris. But what was his *name?*

"I'm—I'm Toby," he murmured in the darkness. "Toby Brubaker."

"Hello, Toby," said a voice.

Toby jumped in fright—

Then he recognized the voice of the Timeling Ariyel.

"Dude!" Toby said. "What a dream I just had!"

"You have not been dreaming," said Ariyel.

Toby sat up and saw Ariyel standing a short distance away, glowing faintly. "What do you mean?" Toby asked.

"You have been in the future," Ariyel said. "Your future. To us Timelings, what you call 'yesterday' or 'tomorrow' is just a different 'now.' All 'nows' are alike to us. I have shown you the now-that-will-be. It is just as real as the now-that-is."

"No way!" Toby said. "It had to be a dream!"

The Timeling said nothing.

Toby's shoulders sagged. He knew Ariyel was telling the truth. "Okay," he said, "so is that what's going to happen to me? Isn't there anything I can do about it?"

"No," Ariyel said. "There is nothing you can do about it."

Toby jumped to his feet and approached the Timeling. "You don't know everything! I can change if I want to!"

"You are powerless to change," Ariyel said. "Greed, theft, selfishness, and lies are a part of who you are, and you can't change that. Can you change your eye color by wishing it were so? It is just as impossible for you to do good after you have become accustomed to doing evil." The Timeling paused. "Besides," he added, "there is the matter of the Dragon's mark."

At the mention of the mark, Toby noticed an itching sensation in the middle of his forehead. He had often felt it, but never paid much attention to it. Suddenly, the place where the Dragon had placed his mark on Toby didn't merely itch—it stung.

Toby clawed at his forehead. If he could have, he would have torn the stinging flesh off his skull. But then Toby realized that it was not the invisible mark in his flesh that condemned him. The mark of the Dragon wasn't just skin-deep. It penetrated into his brain, his mind, his will, his wants, and his emotions. It penetrated to the depths of his soul and his spirit.

"But that's not fair!" Toby cried. "I want to change!"

"You are what you are," Ariyel said. "I'm sorry, Toby. I must leave you now."

"Dude!" Toby screamed. "Don't leave me in the dark again! I'm scared of the dark!"

"I know," Ariyel said, "but this is for your own good. It is only here, in the darkness, that you can see the light." The Timeling began to fade.

"Wait!" Toby said, stumbling toward the Timeling's dim blue form. "Tell me something. Why is God doing this to me? Why does He hate me so much?"

"Hate you?" Ariyel said. "The Creator loves you more than you'll ever know. He sent His Son to die for you. If that isn't love, what is?"

"But if He loves me," Toby said, "then why won't He let me change?"

The Timeling's blue shape had almost completely vanished. "I never said He wouldn't let you change. I said that you cannot change yourself. Nothing is impossible with Him." Then Ariyel was gone.

Toby stood alone in the darkness—and then he realized the darkness that surrounded him seemed safe, almost comforting. *Dude!* he thought. *How come I'm not scared?*

Because I'm with you, a still, quiet voice said within his thoughts.

"God," Toby said, "is that You? This is Toby! Can You hear me?"

This time, Toby didn't hear a voice, but he knew he had

received an answer. The answer washed over him like a wave of love.

"Dude! I mean, God, Sir," he said in a choking voice. "I know I don't deserve any favors. I've made a real mess of everything. I can't blame it on my mom and dad. I can't even blame it on the Dragon. I've got no one to blame but me. But I don't want to end up—I mean, I want to, like, switch sides, okay? I mean, if You'll have me."

And again, that wave of love washed over him.

And Toby said the Name of Jesus, who had died for him. He said the Name again and again. He started walking, shouting the Name over and over. A couple of times, he stumbled, but each time he got back on his feet and continued walking through the darkness, whooping and shouting and laughing.

Soon, he saw a faint blue light up ahead. So he shouted the Name again. Far off in the direction of the light, he heard voices shout back.

"Hey, Grady!" Toby shouted. "Hey, Max! Hey, Allie!"

"Toby!" Grady's voice called back. "We're coming!"

Moments later, Toby saw them coming out of the gloom, surrounded by a shimmering blue glow: Grady in front, followed by Max and Allie, then Mr. O'Dell along with the two Timelings Zaykiel and Jarael. And then he saw Ariyel walking beside him.

Grady ran to Toby, arms spread wide. They slammed into each other, embracing and shouting. Max and Allie joined in, turning the reunion into a group hug.

They led Toby out to the arena of the Fortress, where

Timebender waited. As they walked, Toby told them all that had happened, from his shoplifting misadventure at Merkel's Department Store to seeing his own horrifying future as "Tobias Rex." Even though Grady, Allie, and Max couldn't quite follow all the details, they knew that an incredible change had come over Toby. Even in the dim blue light cast by the Timelings, they could clearly see the look on his face: Toby was genuinely *happy*—maybe for the first time in his life. He had been lost; now he was found. He had died; now he was alive. His old life was gone; his new life was just beginning.

They gathered around Timebender on the floor of the arena—three Timelings and five travelers from Earth. The car was in position for takeoff, pointed toward the Fortress doors.

Max turned to Zaykiel. "What happens now?"

"Now?" the Timeling said. "You all go home, of course."

Grinning broadly, Grady clenched his fist and shouted, "Yes!"

"What about Toby?" Allie said. "He told us about all the things he stole from Merkel's Department Store. When he gets back, he'll be in a lot of trouble with the police."

"Actually," Ariyel said, "I think we can work things out so that it will be as if he never stole those things from Mr. Merkel's store."

"No way!" Toby said excitedly. "If you could do that—Dude, I don't know what to say!"

"Well, what are we waiting for?" Grady said. "Let's go home!"

Max looked worried. "Zaykiel," he said, "can you help us get home?"

"Yes," Zaykiel said, "and sooner than you think."

"What about me?" Mr. O'Dell asked. "I've missed a lot of work because of this trip to Mars. Is there some way you can fix it so that I don't lose money on this deal?"

"Roger O'Dell," Zaykiel said, "these young adventurers have learned some important lessons during this journey. Tell me—what have you learned?"

"I've learned," Mr. O'Dell said, "never to ride in a flying Volkswagen."

"I see," Zaykiel said with a sigh. "Very well, then, I will—as you say—'fix it.' Since money is so important to you, I will make sure you suffer no financial loss. Are you satisfied?"

"Yeah," Mr. O'Dell said, "I'm satisfied."

"All right, then," Zaykiel said, "everyone in the vehicle! Off you go!"

As Toby, Grady, and Mr. O'Dell squeezed into the backseat of the VW, Jarael took Allie aside. "Allie," the Timeling said, "you know that your father will go back to Earth exactly as he was before—nothing is changed. In fact, we will erase all memory of his time on Mars. Do you still think you made the right decision?"

Allie smiled. "I know I did," she said. "He's not exactly

Father of the Year, but he's my dad. I know he loves me—in his own way. I've decided to accept him as he is, and to keep praying for him." Then she got into the car, next to Max.

Once the car doors were closed, the massive doors of the Fortress slowly opened. Pink Martian sunlight filtered into the Fortress. Outside, a dust storm was blowing.

Max didn't even have time to turn on the power. The car started rolling all by itself. It climbed the ramp and rolled through the doors and beyond, where it was swallowed up by clouds of Martian dust.

The Volkswagen climbed above the dust clouds, then shot into space at an astounding speed. Max checked the rearview mirror and saw Mars shrinking behind them. It wasn't long before a bright blue-white pinpoint of light came into view up ahead. It quickly became a blue-and-white marbled disk.

Less than four minutes after they had left Mars, they were descending to Earth. "How did we get here so fast?" Grady asked.

"To get here that fast," Max said, "we had to be traveling at the speed of light! That's impossible!"

From the backseat, Toby laughed. "Dude!" he said. "Nothing is impossible with Him."

Wrapped in its protective blue glow, Timebender sank through the blue skies and silver-white clouds of Earth. The car shot over oceans and mountains like a meteor, then slowed as it descended toward their hometown.

Grady was about to lean forward to say something to Allie when a blue shimmer surrounded her. Surprised,

Grady looked next to him and saw the same blue shimmer surrounding Toby and Mr. O'Dell. An instant later, Allie, her father, and Toby had vanished.

"Hey!" Grady said. "Where did everybody go?"

Max looked around. "Whoa!" he said. "You think they're okay?"

Grady laughed. "Of course they're okay. In fact, I think I know what happened to them. Check your watch— what's the date?"

Max looked at his watch. "Whoa!" he said. "We've arrived back on the same day that this whole crazy adventure began!"

"Awesome!" Grady said. "The Timelings took us back before it all began. Now all Toby has to do is *not* steal that stuff from Merkel's and he's home free!"

"That," Max said, "is totally cool. I'm glad Toby gets a second chance."

"Yeah," Grady said, "and so do we."

"We do?" Max said.

"Yeah," Grady said, laughing. "We get a chance *not* to go to Mars!"

Timebender settled onto the grass in the middle of Max's backyard. Max and Grady opened the doors, got out, and stretched.

"Oh, man!" Grady said. "It's good to be back on good old planet Earth. Hey, what are you doing?"

Max went around to the back of the car and popped the engine cover. "I'm making sure this car never flies again!" he said. He began ripping out parts of his antigravity machine and tossing them on the grass. He took out the ceramic-coated CD and broke it in half. Then he took out the canister of antimatter and set it on the lawn.

"What are you going to do with that canister?" Grady asked.

"I'm going to go to my dad," Max said, "and admit I took it without permission. I probably won't be seeing you for a while—I think this is going to be the biggest grounding of my whole life."

Grady thought for a moment, then he said, "My mom's been after me to clean out the attic. I think I'll go home and do it—and maybe throw in some weeding and mowing."

"Sounds good," Max said, "but don't overdo it. You know how parents are—if you do too much good stuff without being told, they think you're trying to put something over on them."

"Yeah," Grady said. "Hey, it was great going to Mars with you, man."

"Same here," Max said, knocking fists with Grady. "Take care."

Grady waved and took off around the side of Max's house, heading for the street.

Sighing, Max lifted the canister and trudged toward the house. For him, this adventure was over—and the grounding was about to begin. *Still*, he thought, *in a strange sort of way, it feels good doing the right thing, even if it does mean getting grounded. . . .*

In a glassed-in booth overlooking the main floor of Merkel's Department Store, Henry Merkel and Harvey Weems watched the monitors of the store's security cameras. "That's him!" Mr. Merkel said. "That's Toby Brubaker! Zoom in on him! Get this on tape!"

"Right, Mr. Merkel," Harvey Weems said.

The two men watched multiple black-and-white images of Toby Brubaker as he made his way through the electronics department, past displays of computers, scanners, TVs, VCRs, DVD players, stereos, camcorders, and digital cameras. "Oh, he's a slick one, that Brubaker boy," Mr. Merkel said, rubbing his hands together. "He's always—Wait! What's he doing? Where's he going?"

Toby walked out of the electronics department and down the center aisle. As he reached the escalators, he saw Mrs. Purvis step off the escalator with an armload of packages. "Hi, Mrs. Purvis," he said. "Would you like some help with those packages?"

"Why, yes, Toby!" Mrs. Purvis said in surprise. "How nice of you to offer."

Toby took the heaviest packages and followed her out the front door of the store and out into the parking lot.

Meanwhile, up in the glass booth, Mr. Merkel fumed. "Weems!" he said. "Did you see him steal anything?"

"No, sir," Harvey Weems said. "Not a thing."

"Neither did I," Mr. Merkel growled. "But sooner or later, I'll catch him stealing from me again, and then I'll nab him!"

Mr. Merkel could not have been more wrong.

One moment, Allie O'Dell was sitting in the passenger seat of Max McCrane's flying Volkswagen Beetle. The next moment, she was sitting in the passenger seat of her dad's red Jaguar convertible, with the cold wind blowing her hair. Her dad was talking, but Allie didn't catch what he said.

"Excuse me, Dad?" she interrupted. "What were you saying?" She looked at her dad—and was surprised to see that he was clean-shaven. The beard he had worn on Mars was gone. Allie instantly knew what that meant: Time had been reversed.

"I was saying," her father said, "that I have some news for you."

"Oh?" Allie said. "Good news or bad?"

"Well, I think it's good," Mr. O'Dell said. "I hope you'll think so, too."

Allie took a good, close look at her father. He was driving with one hand on the wheel and smiling nervously. He showed no sign that he remembered their adventure on Mars. Just as Jarael had predicted, the Timelings had wiped his memory clean.

"Okay," Allie said. "So what's your big news?"

"Penelope and I are getting married," he said.

Allie held her breath for a moment, then said, "I see."

"You—you don't seem surprised," Mr. O'Dell said.

"Well," Allie said, "you might say I saw it coming. I won't lie to you, Dad. Penelope's not my favorite person in the world, and I can't pretend I'm happy about the marriage—but don't worry about me. I'll be nice and polite."

Mr. O'Dell looked at Allie in surprise. "You will?" He slowed for a stoplight.

"Sure," Allie said. "You have a right to make your own choices—and even your own mistakes."

Mr. O'Dell turned and looked at his daughter. There were tears in Allie's eyes.

"I—I don't know what to say," he said. "I didn't think you'd take it this well."

In a choking voice, Allie said, "Just tell me that, even though you marry someone else, you'll still be my dad." And she added a silent prayer.

Now there were tears in Mr. O'Dell's eyes. He leaned over and gave Allie a kiss on the cheek. "Of course I'll always be your dad," he said, "and I'll always love you."

Allie smiled. "Thank you, Dad," she said. *And thank You,* she prayed.

Behind them, a horn honked loudly. The light was green. Mr. O'Dell gave it the gas, and the Jag leaped forward. Allie and her father continued down the road together.

Three blue Timelings flashed through space at the speed of light. They had just returned five human travelers to their homes. Now, Earth was behind them and Mars shone red before them.

"Well," Jarael said, "that was an interesting assignment."

As they flew, Zaykiel noticed a hundred-thousand-ton asteroid headed for Earth. He quickly calculated the asteroid's speed and trajectory, and saw that it was destined to splash down in the Mediterranean Sea, causing a tidal wave that would kill 2.7 million people. Zaykiel flicked the asteroid away, sending it tumbling toward the Sun.

"What is our next assignment?" Ariyel asked.

"The crew of the Spaceship *Thuvia*," Zaykiel said. "They will be arriving on Mars in forty-two days to investigate the structures at Cydonia. They expect to find evidence of what they call 'extees.'"

"Ah, yes," Jarael said. "Extees. Extraterrestrials. Little green men. Bug-eyed monsters."

"Instead," Ariyel said, "they will find us. But then, I suppose we Emissaries are 'extees' of a sort. After all, we are certainly beings that are not from planet Earth."

"Yes," Zaykiel said. "But I doubt that spirit beings are what they have in mind."

"Shouldn't we reverse time for the crew of Spaceship *Thuvia?*" asked Ariyel. "After all, they have seen Max McCrane's Volkswagen as it flew past them in space. I'm sure they are quite disturbed over the strange mystery of a car on Mars. Perhaps we should erase the past seventeen days from their memories."

"I have already asked Elyon the same question," Zaykiel said. "He told me not to reverse time for the crew. We must leave their memories and experiences as they are."

"Did He explain why?" Ariyel asked.

"No," Zaykiel replied. "But we know that it will all work out for the best—in the Eternal Plan."

"Zaykiel," Jarael said, "you have studied the crew of Spaceship *Thuvia*. Do any of them have the life of Elyon living in them?"

"One of them is a believer," Zaykiel said. "Lia Medina is her name. Another, Thomas Wrye, was raised as a believer, but his faith in Elyon was wounded while he was a university student. His professor once asked him, 'What caused God?' and he didn't have an answer."

"But that question has such a simple answer!" Ariyel said. "'What caused X?' is a question that only has meaning when X had a beginning! The universe had a beginning. Time had a beginning. But Elyon existed before time. In fact, Elyon created time! Therefore, Elyon had no beginning."

"Of course," Zaykiel said. "And that is why the question 'What caused God?' is completely meaningless."

"To Emissaries like ourselves," Jarael said, "the matter is obvious. But such questions easily baffle these poor humans."

"What about the other astronauts aboard Spaceship *Thuvia?*" Ariyel said. "What about Vladimir Kuzmin, Gerard Vachon, Hana Yamada, and Elsa Niemann?"

"They do not believe in Elyon," Zaykiel replied. "Not yet. But I have looked into the now-that-is-to-come."

"And?" Jarael said.

"Soon, they will believe, and they will place their trust in the Name that is above all names," Zaykiel said. "For that is our mission."

The three Timelings hurried on toward Mars, soaring through space at the velocity of love.

Fifty-nine days after leaving the International Space Station, Spaceship *Thuvia* settled into orbit around the Red Planet. A landing craft separated from the main body of the spaceship and descended through the Martian atmosphere. The craft touched down about a half-mile north of the Fortress. Wearing spacesuits and transparent bubble helmets, the six crew members climbed out of the landing craft and set foot on Mars.

The astronauts undocked the Rover, a four-wheeled vehicle loaded with scientific equipment. They climbed aboard and started off toward the Fortress of Cydonia at about ten miles an hour. Over the next three minutes, they steadily approached the massive Fortress. With each passing second, the travelers from Earth became more and more awed by what they saw.

The Fortress was a grim, forbidding castle with walls half a mile high and two miles long. The walls were covered with carvings of horrible reptilian creatures, plus strange scenes of warfare in space, zooming comets, bursting stars, and exploding planets. Over the massive double doors was a replica of the Face on Mars—a face that was both human-like and snakelike, intelligent but inhuman. The carvings of the Fortress were worn by time and blowing sands.

The Rover stopped in front of the huge double doors,

and the astronauts got out. Commander Wrye stared in awe at the Fortress of Evil. Behind him, the rest of the crew gathered in silence—Vladimir Kuzmin, Hana Yamada, Lia Medina, Gerard Vachon, and Elsa Niemann. A Martian breeze whipped up a whirlwind of rust-colored dust.

Then they felt it—a low rumble in the ground, vibrating their boots. Directly in front of them, the massive double doors of the Fortress slowly parted. Out of the darkness, three forms appeared—humanlike but not human. Their bodies glowed with a blue light, and their eyes shone with a golden radiance.

The foremost of the three beings spread his hands in a welcoming gesture. "Greetings, people from Earth," Zaykiel said. "We have been expecting you—and we have much to talk about."

The astronauts exchanged anxious glances.

"Please," Zaykiel said, "do not be afraid." He beckoned to them. "Come."

The three Timelings turned and walked back toward the Fortress. Too astonished to speak, the six astronauts followed.

Their adventure had just begun.

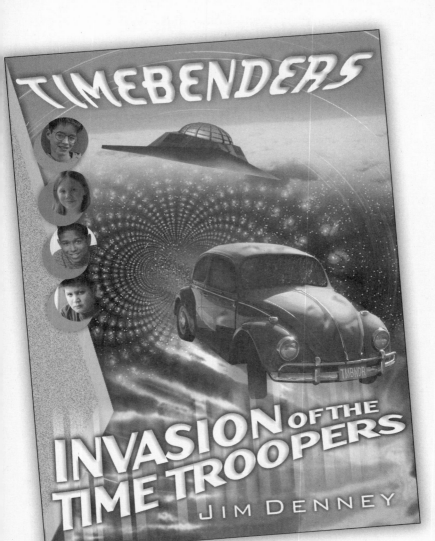

Experience More
Time-Travel Adventures

in

INVASION OF THE
TIME TROOPERS

Excerpt • Timebenders # 3 •
Invasion of the Time Troopers

Grady was staring at something. His eyes were wide and his mouth hung slack. Max and Allie followed Grady's stare and saw—

An orange shimmer on the lawn.

It took shape and solidified into an orange VW Beetle like Timebender. But *this* VW Beetle was different from Timebender in several important ways. For one thing, this VW was dented and bashed, and its windows were cracked and broken. The driver's-side door was missing. Someone had painted bright, colorful designs on the car: rainbows, butterflies, white doves, and flowers—lots and lots of flowers. Along the rear fender, the words FLOWER POWER appeared in bright blue paint.

There were three people in the flowered VW, and they all came tumbling out. The first one came from the driver's side, where the door was missing. She was a red-haired girl with braces. When Allie saw the girl, she gave a shriek. She was looking at *herself!*

The second one out of the car was a lean, athletic-looking African-American with short hair. "You," he said, pointing to the black youth. "You're me! I mean, I'm you! I mean—What's happening?"

Max looked back and forth, from Allie to Allie, from Grady to Grady. Both Allies were dressed exactly alike—denim overalls, pink top, pink scrunchie, white tennis shoes. Both girls had the same freckles, the same braces on their teeth, and the same carrot-red ponytail. It was as if the two Allies were identical twins.

Both Gradys were also dressed exactly alike: baggy blue jeans, a black Tommy Hilfiger shirt, and black Lugz sneakers. With a sense of fear, Max was sure he knew who would emerge next: another Max McCrane.

The third person pushed his way from the back seat of the Volkswagen, tripped on his way out, and went sprawling onto the grass. Max's eyes widened. The third person out of the flowered VW was not Max. It was—

"Toby!" Max said in astonishment. "Toby Brubaker!"

Toby scrambled to his feet. He was a thickset boy, built like a fireplug, with bristly, close-cropped hair, doughy skin, a pug nose, and beady, pale-green eyes. There were pink smears on his face and arms, and his clothes were dirty and grass-stained. Toby Brubaker was no friend of

Max, Allie, or Grady—he had caused them nothing but trouble on their two previous trips in time.

As Max, Allie, and Grady stared in astonishment, the other Allie, the other Grady, and the wide-eyed Toby began shouting and gesturing all at once. They were trying to say something, but it was all a meaningless babble because everybody was yelling at once.

Max, Allie, and Grady stared in shock. They thought this was the most impossible thing that could possibly happen. But in the next instant, something even more impossible happened.

Just a few yards behind the flowered Volkswagen, another shimmer appeared. The shimmers solidified into a strange black-and-white vehicle—a hovercar that floated two feet off the ground. It had a transparent bubble canopy on top. The words TIME TROOPERS were printed on the side of the hovercar in gold letters.

"They found us!" the other Allie screamed.

"Let's get out of here!" the other Grady shouted.

"Aaaaggghhh!" Toby wailed.

The trio jumped back into the flowered VW—Allie in the driver's seat, Grady in the passenger seat, and Toby in back.

Doors opened out of both sides of the black-and-white hovercar. Ramps were lowered to the grass. Men in black-and-white metal armor and helmets walked down the ramps, carrying pistol-shaped devices in their hands. The pistol devices had crystal lenses in front, and reminded Max of laser blasters in a sci-fi movie.

As the armored men stepped onto the grass, Max realized they weren't *men* at all. What at first appeared to be metal armor was actually metal *skin*. The black-and-white metal "men" were actually *robots*.

Each robot had a face of molded steel. Where the eyes should have been were glass disks, like camera lenses. Behind those lenses, pinpricks of cold blue light burned. Where the mouth should have been was a black metal disk, like a radio speaker. Max noticed that each robot had gold lettering on its black-metal chest. On one robot was written: TIME TROOPER 7; on the other: TIME TROOPER 11.

The robots approached the flowered VW, pointing their pistol devices at the three people inside. "Halt!" one of them said in a flat, electronic voice. "Do not engage your time circuits!"

But before the robot had finished speaking, the flowered VW winked out of existence!

"This," said one of the robots, "is getting to be a habit."

The two robots ran back to their hovercar and dashed up the ramps. The doors swung shut. Seconds later, the hovercar winked out of existence.

"What just happened?" Allie asked in a frightened whisper. "Did I just see—me?"

"Yeah," Grady said. "One of them was you, and one of them was me."

"But where was I?" Max asked. "How come there wasn't another me in that car? And why was Toby there instead of me?"

"Guys," Allie said, "I am sooo freaked!"

More Timebender Adventures

Book 1: Battle Before Time

It was our first trip in Timebender, and we were lost. Then, just when I thought I had Timebender headed back to our time, we ended up somewhere before time—*in the middle of a full-scale war!* Planets were blowing up . . . weird lights were whirling all around us . . . we were running out of air . . . and there was no way back! That's when we met a strange new friend who changed our lives forever.

ISBN 1-4003-0039-8

Book 2: Doorway to Doom

An antique doorway . . . a bag of glow-in-the-dark eyeballs . . . and a mysterious intruder from the past. Who would've thought that such a strange combination could create a time transport that would pull me and my friends a thousand years into the past with no way back to our own time?

ISBN 1-4003-0040-1